LITTLE FINGERS

Filip Florian

LITTLE FINGERS

→>-<←

Translated from Romanian by
Alistair Ian Blyth

HOUGHTON MIFFLIN HARCOURT

BOSTON   NEW YORK

2009

Degete Mici by Filip Florian, copyright © 2005 by Filip Florian,
first published in the Romanian language by Editura Polirom
English translation copyright © 2009 by Alistair Ian Blyth

For information about permission to reproduce selections from this book,
write to Permissions, Houghton Mifflin Harcourt Publishing Company,
6277 Sea Harbor Drive, Orlando, Florida 32887-6777.

www.hmhbooks.com

Library of Congress Cataloging-in-Publication Data
Florian, Filip.
[Degete mici. English]
Little fingers / Filip Florian ; translated from Romanian by Alistair Ian Blyth.
p. cm.
ISBN 978-0-15-101514-6
1. Mass burials—Romania—Fiction. 2. Archaeologists—Fiction.
3. Anthropologists—Fiction. 4. Anti-communist movements—Fiction.
5. Romania—Fiction. I. Blyth, Alistair Ian. II. Title.
PC840.416.L64D4413 2009
859'.335—dc22   2008050564

Book design by Linda Lockowitz

Printed in the United States of America

DOC 10 9 8 7 6 5 4 3 2 1

With thanks to the Romanian Cultural Institute for their generous financial support.

To Mirela,
who makes the best coffee in the world.
Her laugh makes me melt.

CHAPTER ONE

Among the monks, disciples, and workers at Red Rock (and more than twenty souls had gathered since the coming of summer, when they began to paint the church murals and shingle the roof), that young man, one of the carpenters' mates, always with rolled-up trousers and sawdust in his eyebrows, was the first to see the bluish-black tuft. He had returned from town at a run, where he had been sent to fetch a new saw blade, a chisel, and some glue. He did not stop at the scaffolding or the huts, but kept on climbing. He found the priest in the upper part of the clearing, on the sunny slope where he always read after lunch and, out of breath, the boy told him the terrible tidings from the fort. Onufrie watched how he panted, how he gesticulated as though he were groping for the words with his hands, he listened to him speaking awkwardly, with long pauses, about a torrent of human bones that had not fallen from the heavens like rain, but emerged from the earth near a subsided wall. He did not ask any questions; he did not interrupt. He slowly removed his straw hat and, closing his eyes, making three broad signs of the cross, clutched it to his chest. The disciple too had crossed himself, abruptly falling silent, not because he had nothing else to say, but because after one such great shock, the second struck him dumb. The tar-black locks rose from the priest's crown, alien to his sleek, creamy white hair, and then began to discolor, to wilt like frost-nipped flowers, leaving a purplish ichor to flow. After a while, which may have been half a minute or a quarter of an hour, Onufrie adjusted his hat on his head, pushed it back toward the nape of his neck, and thrice shook his forefinger at the valley, reiterating that *Thrice has the Mother of God descended from the Heavens to show Her succor and faith.* He hastened to his hut to fetch surplice, stole, and censer, then went into the small chapel for a few candles and, pushing the boy from behind as if he were a lame sheep, Onufrie set off to see what there was to be seen, and to scatter incense over the bones at the Roman fort.

CHAPTER TWO

→>−<←

X, A DAILY PAPER FOR NEWS, OPINION, and analysis, no. 1712, July 3, Y, 16 pages, Z lei, Investigations section, article "Victims Increase, Prosecutors Tight-lipped":

> Yesterday, four new victims were recorded on the edge of spa resort W. Given the pace at which human remains are being exhumed and classified, it is clear that the death toll of the executions ordered by party chiefs in the past will exceed 100 or even 150. The mass grave — discovered by chance on the first day of the school holidays by the children we featured in one of our previous articles — appears to be a bottomless pit.
>
> The attitude of the military prosecutors, who refuse to accept the evidence, continues to be suspect. If the method of establishing the number of dead by the number of skulls has been accepted, it is incomprehensible why there is no public acknowledgment that this was death by firing squad. However, there are hints that the prosecutors and along with them the coroner taking part in the inquiry might reconsider their position. Yesterday, for the first time, on the orders of Magistrate Colonel Spiru, the officials responsible for the investigations ceased to provide any more statements to the press. In comparison with the attempt to ascribe an earlier date to the terrible mass grave in W and, implicitly, to absolve the secret police of any blame, silence — this *si-*

lenzio stampa that the forensic investigators have imposed on themselves like the footballers of the national team—would seem to be a step forward. It is possible that from now on the murderers, their commandants, and their accomplices still in high office might not be protected so zealously.

For the time being, the only representative of an important institution who confirms that this was a political crime remains the chief of local police, Major Maxim, interviewed on numerous occasions by our newspaper. He has single-handedly made efforts to go back in time, to the 1950s and '60s, in order to seek out the murderers: those who pulled the triggers and those who gave the orders. His latest declaration, which the major has offered to us exclusively, is as follows: "A very great deal of pressure is being put on me to give up. I won't give up. Regardless of the risks. There are so many human lives, children, too . . ."

→><+-

As for the closure of the archaeological site (which, around the middle of April had reached the perimeter of the armory), Major Maxim was responsible for that too—the hominid bell pepper, as he had been dubbed by a usually taciturn research student. The same student, who was researching the equipment and battle techniques of the North Danube legions, had sketched, after three shots of rum, a portrait of the cop: bushy mustache, crafty eyes, a gut that gestated not quadruplets, only flatulence. The major had ordered the cessation of all activity in the fort area after a young lad of eleven, while looking for worms to fish for barbels, had found a skull that did not look like either a dog's or a goat's. Although the mass grave was situated far from the Roman site, more than three hundred feet away, the chief of police had proved hostile to the idea of synchronizing forensics with heuristics, and he had not permitted excavation of the furnace and the adjacent rooms to proceed in tandem with his investigations. The opinion of the professor in charge of the dig, who dated the bones at around 1800, did nothing to dull the zeal of Major Maxim, nor even stir any doubt in him, though the professor had seen more ancient and medieval tombs than the latter had caught pickpockets. In any case, the former, a university man up to his eyes in research, conferences, books in progress, lectures, and bilious attacks, had departed soon after that episode, leaving it to the others to enlighten a turbid mind, and saying: "Boys, I don't have the time for pickling, so why don't you deal with the bell pepper and call me when he's done!" However, the officer, who couldn't have cared less about centurions' swords, chain mail, lances, helmets, daggers, shields, crossbows, catapults, and whatever else might lie beneath the earth, had not let them put him in brine or vinegar; instead, he was the one who singed them over a low flame, like eggplants for a chutney. In order to permit the archaeological site to reopen, he demanded an explanatory document regarding the dozens, perhaps hundreds of dead bodies, which had turned up in his precinct. On three different occasions (picking wax out of one ear, smoothing his mustache, tightening his tie knot), he had declared to the archaeologists that a few rusty bits of tin meant nothing next to so many human bones.

First some sergeants and warrant officers had shown up, who guarded the ruins day and night and drove away the curious; later they set about carting the bones to police headquarters in a wheelbarrow covered with tarpaulin sheeting. The ground was friable and the bones came loose easily. Initially the soldiers had worked with shovels and spades, even with hoes (many of them were accustomed to digging up potatoes and turnips), but then they had switched to gentler tools. They dug with builder's trowels and putty knives; they cleaned each bone with soft brushes, rather like paintbrushes. Things were worse when it rained, because then each excavation filled up with water. "Look at them wallowing in the mire," someone remarked during a shower. "You'd think they were pigs." And that was about right. The person who had spoken (with a teacup between his palms) and his colleague (munching toast) gazed from the veranda of the cabin (the archaeologists' house, as it was called in town), while the gendarmes, wearing raincoats and rubber boots over their uniforms, tramped through the mud and scrabbled in the clayey earth. They had given up on the putty knives and brushes. They poked around directly with their fingers and rinsed the bones in puddles. One or another would sometimes slip and fall, but this happened rarely: as a rule they tripped each other, they shoved each other, they came up with all kinds of tricks to topple those who had managed to stay clean. This practice, prompted by the rain, ceased as soon as Magistrate Colonel Spiru made his appearance.

When it rained, those watching from the veranda would go into the small room of the cabin, the only room, which served as a cloakroom, storeroom, dining room, office, and much more, and they would try to find themselves a chair among the jumble of that cramped space. They would wait for something to boil in the coffee pot on the Primus, maybe some milk, maybe some wine with sugar and spices. Once, during a chilly shower, a drenched captain had striven to smile and seek shelter, but he had been recommended to buy an umbrella. If the archaeologists were forbidden to research the armory of the fort, then at least, they felt, they should be able to enjoy the show in the company of whom they pleased. Among the few who were welcome there was the coroner, ever amazed at the virulence of the accounts concerning Major Maxim, who, the coroner believed, had guzzled so many onions that his brain had seized up; Mr. Sasha, the photographer, who used to tether his dromedary to the small handrail of the steps; Titus Maeriu, the representative of former political prisoners at the exhumation of those unknown bones; a few journalists, who inclined toward the version of a Communist massacre, but had grasped that the chief of police was aiming at an advancement in rank; Mrs. Embury's niece, with all her freshness; and a biologist from the town, who was also prone to irrepressible outbursts against the major. From the cabin, they followed the events at the mass grave, without missing a single detail. They witnessed, for example, the transportation of the bones back from police headquarters, a return journey devoid of glory. The bones were carted back by the same sergeants and warrant officers, in a wheelbarrow once again, except that this time they had lost their air of cocks strutting among hens. They resembled trembling sparrows who did not know how to vanish quickly enough from the sight of an old tomcat that was as yet indulgent, a tomcat with prominent cheekbones and a colonel's insignia. They approached slowly, perhaps because of the gradient and the weight, they emptied the wheelbarrow where they were ordered, and hurried away. Because their trips were repeated and it was never clear whether the scene was unfolding for the last time, hefty bets had been laid in the cabin, from which betting the taciturn doctoral student had won almost a quarter of a month's wages. Then the archaeologists were witness to the "great inventory," which had commenced with the placement of four folding tables at the sides of the mass grave, and next to it the prosecutors lined up. Under the supervision of Colonel Spiru, the magistrates distributed to the soldiers transparent bags of different sizes, for the femur to the tarsus and the tibia to the sacrum, to which, on their return, were attached white labels with a code number and a few basic observations. They were interested in whether they could identify traces of bullets; they put question marks next to any broken or fissured skulls that could be argued to have suffered blows.

Returning for a moment to the coroner, it would chance that he sometimes made more placid appearances at the archaeologists' house. As a rule, his good moods were the result of nights at the hotel, when he was visited by a lady journalist fond of red wines and the gentle thrusts of his bottom, which was broader than his shoulders, at the end of which he used to sleep soundly. And in one of those relaxed, matutinal moments, subsequent to cabernet and tactile ardor, he had come up with the idea that the military magistrates were assiduously working on a huge puzzle, with thousands or tens of thousands of pieces. "How is that?" someone had asked, in passing, unsuspecting as to what would follow: a lengthy and convoluted description, in which the coroner imagined the mass grave being emptied and all the bodily remains spread out on the grass by the prosecutors, filling the entire area of the fort. He imagined Colonel Spiru strolling among them, hands behind his back, now and then picking up a bone and attempt-

ing to discover its correspondent, more often than not getting
the match wrong, losing his temper and punishing the hapless
gendarmes with orders to lie down and then stand to attention,
or to do push-ups, then proceeding on his way, as if through a
labyrinth, ever more rapidly and more confused, not at all prepared to give up, dreaming of a finale in which the reassembled
skeletons would stand all in a row, dozens, perhaps hundreds,
each perfectly reconstructed, with not a single element missing
and in no case with a humerus or even a metacarpus positioned
anywhere other than in its proper place. In reply, a voice from
the cabin had proposed a game of baccarat or poker. And there
had been plenty of takers.

→>◄+-

All those who had been unable to resist the temptation of writing
a monograph on their town—a teacher, a lawyer, two monks,
a veterinarian, and a stationmaster—had lived in the conviction that, after the Roman fort had been abandoned (or burned
down or succumbed to an annihilating plague or been smitten
by God), the earth had swallowed it up once and for all. They
believed that layers of sand, clay, divers sediments, and black
earth had accumulated down the ages, thickly, densely, over the
principia, thermae, canabae, and *horreum*; they told themselves
that a carnal, aggressive vegetation had overrun the hills. Having established the origins of the town and its first documentary attestations, the authors of those amateur chronicles set
the ruins to one side until 1932, when, they recorded, an en-
thusiastic team of archaeologists brought to light a number of
crumbled walls. The event was succinctly recorded, but what
seemed to impress them was not the emergence of the ruins,

their coming to light after two millennia of darkness, but the presence of a special creature among the group of professors and students. There were hostile or admiring (in no case neutral) references to that personage. In the work by the lawyer, Stratulat, alongside a charcoal portrait, one finds a detailed description of a woman with closely cropped hair, always dressed in jodhpurs and riding boots, the owner of an eight-inch-long amber cigarette holder. She was a matchless speaker of French, one discovers from the text of the schoolmaster, she moved slowly, roundly, she authoritatively kept in check the day laborers hired for the dig, while from her vaporous blouses there wafted the scent of figs. Gavrilescu, the veterinarian, compared her to a crested mountain hen with puffed-up feathers, capable of provoking savage fights between cocks during the mating season. The railway man had seen her traveling in the deluxe sleeping cars of the express, always accompanied by elegant gentlemen (often including a minister and a general), who used to expend their surplus passion at the roulette and baccarat tables of the casino. From the texts of the teacher and the father abbot, on the other hand, there erupts irritation and lamentation over the fact that, in the summer and autumn of that year, the younger generation or, in the wider sense, the flock of the faithful, was disposed to fall into evil ways. The teacher was vexed that at the girls' school there had spread the fashion of cutting the hair in a fringe and lopping off pigtails, that the pupils of the lower school and the lycée were jostling to take part as volunteers, during lessons and not only then, in unearthing the ancient buildings. And Archimandrite Macarius maliciously noted that the number of patresfamilias in church for holy liturgy was falling alarmingly and that the tranquility of many couples, to judge from the content of confessions, was imperiled. The only one who consummately ignored that exotic being and the occurrences she gave rise to, the only one from whose text one would not even have been able to deduce that the charming Amazon had ever been born was the other monk, Father Ioanichie. As the proponent of theories of purely Old Testament provenance, he did not doubt that upon the town there had once simultaneously descended the wrath of the Father and that of the Son, united in devastating and purifying force—a wrath capable of covering up with flowers, bushes, and trees a place of infamies between men for seventeen centuries. And this servant of the Lord, whose grave lay among those of the ordinary monks in the courtyard of the monastery, had been certain that the unearthing of the first stone of the old fort signaled a reawakening of the evil, of the vice that he for one had detected in the gestures and appetites of his flock.

I found the six monographs in a nook of the public library, at the end of a week's search. My good fortune came simultaneously with an ulcer attack, because it was only the signs of pain on my ashen face that, after a number of failed attempts, finally awakened some kind of solidarity in the bitter sadness of the lady who administered the institution. With an expression of complicity, Mrs. Mia (as she introduced herself to me) had extracted the key chain that dangled between her huge breasts. Belabored by her obesity, she had unlocked the door to a small room, subject like all the others to the influence of that climate without seasons in such spaces—musty air, a mixture of dust, macerated paper, and cockroach poison. It was a narrow box room intended for brooms, mops, and gas canisters, but it had not fulfilled its destiny. What I saw before me, behind a curtain of spider webs and mouse droppings, represented an old bequest of the town hall (the living memory of the locality, the fat lady whispered to me). It was comprised of orders of the day from the guard regiment; plans of monuments; visitors' books from the sanatorium, casino, and hotels; posters for charity balls; bequeathal documents, registration certificates, and the last wills of prominent persons; the programs of coastal automobile races; Scout and Guard hymns; council decisions regarding the naming of main streets; and designs for buildings never constructed, such as a theater, a skating rink, and a hermitage at St. Veronica's grotto. Amid the plans, registers, and files, it took me an entire morning and half a tube of antacid to extract the manuscripts of which I expected so much from heaps of yellowing documents. By the end of this operation, my checked shirt had turned a uniform gray, my mouth and nostrils were clogged up with a mealy, brackish dust, and the notion of soap and a hot bath seemed more tempting than ever. In my naivety, I had imagined that I would study the hundreds of pages in peace and quiet, with toast and marjoram tea to hand, tunes by the Mills Brothers softly flowing in the background, and a hot water bottle on my tummy, while I stretched out on the soft, restful bed in the room I rented from Auntie Paulina. However, as I rummaged for hours on end, what little goodwill the librarian may once have had soon vanished, and pickled bitterness once more laved her features. She fixed me with her beady eyes, set deeply between puffy eyelids, and, breathing with difficulty, panting asthmatically, she informed me that the rare items from the special collection could be consulted only in the reading room.

I had chosen the best-lit spot, next to a south-facing window, and I pored over those forgotten texts in usually unpleasant company, made up of Mrs. Mia's friends and pensioners filling in lottery tickets. I hoped to discover some old event or at least a clue regarding the bones among the ruins. I was dealing with scripts that were not at all similar, from the meticulous, excessively calligraphic handwriting of the former abbot to the rebellious, barely legible hand of the veterinarian. Topic and orthography also differed, likewise narrative style, but overall there was a nagging common basis, a tacit understanding on the part of the chroniclers to treat the same events polemically. The stationmaster, for example, ascribed the cancellation of a visit by Franz Joseph at the beginning of the century to a plot by Hungarian railway workers. The teacher saw in the sudden change of imperial schedule a lesson for King Carol I. Dr. Gavrilescu explained the incident by the incompatibility of the date of the journey with the foxhunting season. And the lawyer Stratulat presumed that the decision of the Viennese court was due to amorous reasons, impossible to include in an official communiqué. On this matter, in spite of their placement at such distant rungs of the ecclesiastical ladder, Macarius and Ioanichie nonetheless coincided in their convictions, interpreting the gesture of the last Hapsburg as a Roman Catholic infamy flung in the face of Orthodoxy. As for the facts that interested me, facts upon which the continuation of research at the Roman fort depended, I suspected that if I did not find information in one of the texts, then it would be missing in all the others. But between the dark-brown wrappers that protected the jurist's version there was nothing that explained the presence of dozens of skeletons within the perimeter of the fort. I had reached the end of that account one Wednesday. I remember it precisely, because people were coming back from the stadium after a cup match. It was getting on toward six o'clock, closing time, and, since I had neglected my lunch of rusks and cottage cheese, my stomach was giving me hell. The throbbing of my ulcer and my evident disappointment once more mollified the librarian, who felt the need, in the empty room, to sit down beside me and rattle on about the fugue of mankind's books. The sun had been dwarfed and was just about to vanish behind a wooded peak when I felt her clammy fingers between my legs.

I could not abandon reading the rest of the manuscripts, the stakes were too high, but under the new circumstances, I was dependent upon the schedule of others. Whenever the reading room was empty, I avoided going in, and when the last patrons left, I would hasten to accompany them. The fat lady, although she often wore glasses, rhomboid ones on a gilt cord, behaved after that embarrassing episode as though I were transparent. Her feigned indifference had something menacing about it, but, in comparison with the stubbornness of the chief of police or the unyieldingness of the former political prisoners and journalists who had arrived from Bucharest, it seemed child's play. Those aged gentlemen, tortured and at the same time fascinated by the past, along with the young journalists, belated anti-Communists, could not accept that the host of bodily remains was anything other than the consequence of a summary execution perpetrated at the edge of a mass grave in the 1950s. They were not interested in the opinion of the historians. The coroner's hesitancy seemed suspect to them, the fruit of cowardice. Even the fact that the prosecutors had not identified a single bullet was regarded as a sign of complicity, decades later, with the authors of the massacre. They were faithful to their own theory, one that spawned categorical commentaries and articles in the press. In their view, the absence of teeth proved torture preliminary to shooting. The cracked skulls were perceived as evidence that pistol butts and clubs had been employed. The position of the limbs at a certain distance from the collarbones and pelvises demonstrated that it had not been a case of Christian burial, but that the lifeless bodies had been tumbled down together from a height. The man of the moment was Major Maxim, and he was tireless in granting interviews to the dailies, weeklies, news agencies, radio stations, and television channels. His flair as a policeman, his uncommon professional feeling (as he himself constantly claimed) told him that we were faced with an odious crime, which would not go unpunished. In order to convince the film cameras, but also the microphones and dictaphones, the major would ceaselessly run his fingers over his blackish mustache, clench his jaws, and, in a grave voice, demand understanding for the discretion his investigations imposed. As for the monographs, the possible source whereby to quell the controversies, they neglected medieval necropolises and showed no interest at all in the places where ancestors had been laid to eternal rest. The veterinarian made uncertain reference to an outbreak of horse sickness, which was supposed to have mowed down some of the most svelte steeds before the first princely lieutenancy, but he gave no information at all about the early placement of a cemetery between the fortress walls.

What on earth would I have done if Auntie Paulina had not told me her dreams every morning, as she and I lounged in the wicker rocking chairs on the veranda with tea and slices of walnut cake, with the ceaseless drizzling rain, the radio low in the background. It was cozy, torpid, although a little chilly. The marjoram tea never had sugar in it, but luckily there was walnut cake aplenty. Besides, her stories did not bother me at all. I was not one of the protagonists, I merely listened, a witness to occurrences imagined or experienced by others. I had deliberately lost my watch in the laundry basket. I used to put my hands over my ears whenever some radio announcer gave the exact time.

What did time matter when Auntie Paulina was being visited frequently, almost regularly, by a man in a tailcoat, white silk shirt, and garnet red bow tie? A middle-aged man, slightly graying, with freshly shaven cheeks, on the tall side, with no trace of physical weakness, a man in the full sense of the word. I only had to think of the forever fresh bouquet of cornflowers, blue to match her eyes, that he would gallantly present to her, smelling them before placing them in her lap, and that was enough for me to be able to understand. Unfortunately, there was still a clock ticking in my stomach (who knows when I had swallowed it), one I could not stop. I would grow hungry. (Ah, how much I hated that!) I would bite my tongue, delay declaring it aloud. I would be burning inside. The ulcer was always the bitterest foe of dialogue, but I would endure it for a time, while the gentleman ceremoniously invited her, in accordance with all the rules of etiquette, for a ride in a limousine, a 1932 Plymouth, never any other make or year of manufacture, a ride on the highway. Where the notion of a highway came from God only knows, as such a thing had never existed in the town. It's possible that the gentleman might have known of one, I don't doubt it. So, a ride on the highway, with the engine in first gear, slowly, gently, alongside the pavement, not from a spirit of caution but so that all might see Auntie Paulina and the company she keeps. I said that I was going to the bathroom, just a moment, excuse me. I hurried to the kitchen and munched two or three bits of toast, not even half a slice, everything turned rosy, and the motorcar seemed to be entering the park. The chauffeur solemnly opened the doors, I don't think it would have been possible without him, a young, blond man in a gray suit and a peaked cap. The couple alighted in a studied fashion, casting casual looks around them. They leisurely headed down the lane, treading the faded chestnut leaves underfoot (it was always autumn), toward the stand where the brass band was playing. The gentleman bestowed money on the beggars, absorbed in the conversation, not for a moment casting his eyes at the outstretched hands to his left and right. And she fluttered her eyelashes and with lips slightly pouting, just enough to make an impression, whispered romantic words about migratory birds. There was even a discreet squeeze of the arm or two—accidentally, of course. The music was drawing closer, it seemed linked to the mechanical greetings, the oblique movements of their heads became ever more frequent around the bandstand. Unknown figures, respectable and at the same time respectful, and among the ragged, unwashed wretches at the edges (to crown it all) who do you think! Mioara, the pharmacist, Paraschiva, with her walking stick, and Jenny: "My neighbors, dear, looking in a sorry state." Then came the elegant beau monde, a series of strangers, always different ones, and around about, beside them, the acquaintances of youth. They sprang up in the uniforms of the Iron Guard, of watchmen, of maltreated soldiers or, worse still, full-grown men with white hair dressed in school uniforms. And again I would say that I needed to go to the bathroom: "Probably a cold, Auntie Paulina, what can you expect with all this rain, I'll be right back." In the kitchen once again, a transparent slice of cheese, a mouthful of boiled egg. In the bandstand, the conductor bowed reverently, the music continued to play, and the two vacant chairs in the middle waited for the couple to be seated. No one else would have dared to take them. There was applause between the melodies. The gentleman, by innocent mistake, touched her high-heeled snakeskin shoe, immediately withdrew his own lacquered one. The incident, let us call it a happy one, passed with a slight flush of the cheeks. There was applause. They too applauded. Their shoes met once more, sometimes even their shoulders. The street lamps were lighted, the sky became ruddy, the conductor sought their gaze and did not omit to bow low once more (it was always autumn), and a chill settled over the music. I was dreaming of chicken soup and the noodles therein. They were in the limousine again, she with a navy blue mohair shawl over her blue dress. Lights were multiplying in the town, were shining, on the rear seat it was dark, the chauffeur was looking ahead, impenetrably, the gentleman, sitting with his palms decorously on his knees, was recounting

the life of an illustrious Italian tenor. My stomach was burning
unbearably, I'm hungry, Auntie, I'm hungry, Ah, oh dear, it's a
good thing you said so, I had got carried away by the story.

Sitting in the wicker rocking chair I had once listened to
Auntie Paulina's dream of how a woman with red hair cast a
spell on Virgil, Paulina's nephew. The woman had removed his
wedding ring without him feeling it. Then she had knotted a
lock of her hair on the ring, a lock cut from the right temple.
She circled it seven times over the man's heart and then placed
it in his palm. Virgil disappeared. Then Paulina saw him walking on a tall bridge, somewhere very high up, over a river. He
had kept glancing to the side, never downward at the tumult
of waters. Bitter tea, walnuts from the cake, glazed with burnt
sugar. The woman with red hair had re-appeared out of no-
where. She was dancing, holding her arms crosswise as though
she were clutching a partner to her chest. Virgil, motionless,
was looking in the other direction, and only his profile could
be made out. The dance made a detour around him. Of the
woman there had remained only the scent of wormwood. And
nonetheless the tea had an exceptional aroma; few plants conceal such a virtue. The floor shook, the floor too was dancing,
the river turned red, ever darker, until it took on the hue of the
woman's locks. At last Virgil trod on the solid ground, among
flowers, thousands of flowers. The sun rose from many places
at once. There had been six, to count them, six suns against the
sky. A few days before, the postman had brought a letter from
Virgil's mother, Lucica, Auntie's younger sister. I had read it,
in my impossible voice. When I was a child, Father used to say
I spoke as though I were munching berries. Paulina had lost
her glasses, now she was listening. Virgil had fallen asleep in

the bath with the faucet flowing. The water had lapped as far as the electric radiator that was heating the room, and the fuse had blown. What luck, eh! Virgil had been burned where the skin is most delicate, which is to say where? Just a moment, Auntie Paulina, it says here, look, between the legs and under the armpits. I bet the poor boy would have preferred an ulcer. It doesn't matter, dearest, at least he escaped with his life, these dreams . . .

→►◄←

In the afternoons, I went out. It would be drizzling, I would cross the road toward the Roman fort, the water would gush down at every step. Sooner or later I would raise the collar of my overcoat. The path seemed to have been forgotten since the archaeological dig had been broken off. A dry wind was always blowing among the walls of the fort. I could feel it somewhere in my bones.

→►◄←

The gentleman rose up again, the frock coat, the bouquet of cornflowers, the brass band, the limousine, the two of them alone on the seat in the back. A click of the fingers, the chauffeur opened a bottle of French champagne, crystal glasses, the monotonous thrum of the motor, traffic lights. The gentleman calmly threw his bow tie out of the window, unfastened the top two buttons of his shirt, hummed a chansonette. She was melting like a wax candle. The young man at the wheel was looking fixedly ahead; his neck seemed immobile. Two antacid pills. I would give anything to avoid an operation. Outside town. A forest. In the beam of the headlights there stretches a rustling yellow glade. The chauffeur is playing a violin stowed until then in the trunk. A tango, they float together, the soles of their shoes crush the dry leaves. She takes fright on hearing the screeches of some cranes (it is always autumn). The headlights fade, the stars are wholly absent, the violin weeps, a pity that the gentleman will not for anything in the world renounce decorum. "You urinate rather frequently, dear," Auntie Paulina scolds me as I am gulping down a rusk or a ripe apple in the kitchen. The chauffeur abandoned in the field at night, houses on either side of the road. The motorcar, a 1932 Plymouth, never any other make or year of manufacture, judders, takes flight, the gentleman impassively observes that the brakes have gone, it descends an endless sloping street, how wonderful it would have been if it had had wings. How about a beef stew today? And it was not autumn, but late June.

On the morning when a hubbub of car horns and a brass band invaded the town, I was reading the pages of Ioanichie the monk. I abandoned his story of the wolves that used to circle the monastery in winter. (A description of wild beasts as servants of the devil: they would run madly along a single track, as numerous as lice, making not a path but a trench as deep as the foundations of the walls, wanting to undermine them. Then they would collapse exhausted, gather fluffy snow with their long snakelike tongues, revive, and set off to gnaw the gates with fangs as sharp as tailors' needles and claws as sharp as razors. Some would ram the grooved oak beams with the crowns of their heads, because it was precisely there, under the bristling fur, that they had grown horns.) On the first floor, from one of the windows of the public library, I watched the strange procession on the main street. The individual with a felt hat, borne like a soloist on the hood of a car, seemed to be Luci, the one who had just mown the grass in Lady Embury's yard. But what was that music?

In one of the secret places whence the angels watch over the world so that our Lord God may know everything (theater boxes upholstered with forest moss, suspended from the stars like balloon baskets, willow-wood watchtowers planted in the high heavens and pointing to the ground, superimposed upon the solar disk so that the dazzled eyes of mortals will not sense their presence), neither the persistence of so many motorcar horns nor the din of drums, cymbals, and trumpets can have passed unobserved. The noise was coming from down the hill, from near the train station or farther away, from the TB sanatorium, and in the warm pre-prandial air it caused a number of things to occur. Quiet strolls were interrupted. Hotel balconies became animated. The torpor of taxi drivers and summer-terrace waiters evaporated. Vendors emerged from shops, from candy and souvenir stalls, from the ice cream and opera glass kiosks in front of the cinema. Vacationing children abandoned antiquated optical devices trained on the mountains. At the entrance to the park, next to the dromedary decked in oriental trinkets, Mr. Sasha, the photographer scanned the horizon through dark glasses, trying to detect something in the bend to the right of the post office, where the raucous convoy would have to appear. For the benefit of the girls from the lycée waiting on a bench for the No. 3 bus, the one that goes to the waterfall, Mr. Sasha launched the hypothesis that for breakfast at the sanatorium they had put gas in the tea of the lung patients instead of bromine.

Then, at the bottom of the boulevard, there emerged an unusual coach and four: a gleaming white Mercedes drawing a hearse that once would have been drawn by horses. Behind it came other cars with headlights lit and mourning ribbons tied to the side mirrors. They advanced slowly, with a kind of highway-code piety, but it was hard to say where they were heading, given that church and cemetery were now behind them. No priest accompanied the cortege. Instead, the driver of the lead limousine, using a megaphone, was singing "Eternal Remembrance" in a strangulated falsetto. The first to remark upon this was Mrs. Photiade, the pharmacist, who called upon the aid of the Holy Virgin for the peace of all. It was also she who recognized the man at the wheel and, turning pale, biting her lips with her small catlike teeth, she had withdrawn into the laboratory, among the test tubes and healing substances.

At the windows of the motorcars, the brass and percussion instruments gleamed in the late June light like gold leaf, as the blowers and drummers wielded them passionately, like an old-style ragtime band. What rose from the column was not a funeral march. The notes pummeled each other, jittered and ricocheted all over the place. They clashed heads like rams, in a deafening racket. Of the mob of occasional musicians (money changers, pimps, thugs with knuckle dusters), Luci, in possession of the tuba, was the only one who sought a measure of delicacy. When the white Mercedes pulled up in front of the town hall and the long line, like a corpulent, endless worm, came to a halt, it was Luci who lent nobility to the minute's silence. The car alarms and horns had died down. The band had fallen silent. And Luci, sitting cross-legged on the hood of a jeep, with one of his elegant hats pulled over his eyebrows, his silver earring glinting in his left earlobe, strove to capture something that may, in the absence of an oboe, have been a snatch of Marcello's concerto in D minor. There was silence all around, even too much silence, except for Aladdin, the dromedary, who kept bellowing.

As for the hearse, one might say that it was a fine one. It had chubby cherubs engraved on its frontispiece, biblical scenes on the sides, and cherry-red drapes tied back with braid. It had been affected by rain and too many last journeys; the paint was peeling and birds, mice, and insects had left their mark in a multitude of holes and fissures. It reeked of pee, because until lately a bitch and her pups had been sheltering inside it. In front of this lugubrious conveyance, a few of the men lit cigars; one of them was smoking a pipe. They lifted out the coffin, bore it with slow steps, and placed it on a metal stand at the very entrance to the town hall. At the head of the coffin, they arranged a voluminous object, shrouded in a sheet, and two small wreaths of yellow dandelion flowers.

The driver of the Mercedes (wearing flip-flops, tight shorts, and a Chicago Bulls T-shirt bulging over his belly) conducted the funerary rite, fervently crying "Lord have mercy." At his signal, but without neglecting their tobacco, the men hastened to unveil the cross and lift the lid off the coffin. A murmur spread among the onlookers, such as occurs when the relief of a crowd blends with amazement or livelier excitement. Between the pine planks, with arms crossed over its chest, its legs crooked and bandy, there lay a life-size doll, made of rags and straw, dressed in a tatty suit. It had a broad face, smothered by a beard. On the cross at its head there was pasted an election poster, showing a beaming candidate, confident in his powers, while beneath, on a plaque, there was inscribed "Here rests Victor Lazu, a shit who wanted to be mayor."

⤙⤙

Mr. Lazu teaches biology. Here is a description of him one Tuesday morning: his skin, like that of all inveterate smokers, has a gray cast. The dark rings around his eyes do not look as though they have been caused by insomnia or the flu. His long hair, sprouting from the temples, always falls to the sides exposing his bare pate. His thin beard has snatched away his air of an impassioned and obdurate officer in the White Army (this is the opinion of a lady, a pharmacist, who many years after their separation is still unmarried). The bushy eyebrows have remained unchanged, like the slightly hooked nose, the fleshy lips and beveled cheeks (features for which the pharmacist still preserves, in a drawer of her dressing table, under her lingerie, a scratched Tom Jones record, to the melodies of which they had once danced).

In the company of the photographer (the dromedary is outside the café, tethered to a metal pole) Mr. Lazu is drinking glass after glass of bitters, and talking about the chief of police. Mr. Sasha has a bottle of beer and a bag of chips in front of him; he is listening. Both are sitting with their chins propped on their palms, one elbow resting on the table, one man with the right, the other with the left. Music is flowing over them; groups and singers whom Pusha the barmaid has been hoping will drive away her toothache. In the gaps between CDs, quite a few things can be heard. Firstly: ". . . should have sent a sergeant major to sort it out, what the hell! He would have nabbed them for disturbing the peace, for loitering, for what-

ever, dished out a few fines. There are spas here, people who
are ill. They come here to rest, not to get high blood pressure. You would have seen how the whelps would have qui-
eted down if Maxim had raised a finger, but he didn't want to,
I'm telling you, he didn't want to, that's clear!" After that (and
on Mr. Lazu's forehead a thin, bluish blood vessel is pulsat-
ing, like a river of lesser cartographic importance): ". . . and he
was blathering nonsense upon nonsense to me about the bones,
about expert opinions. As big as he is, with that gut of his, at
one point he bends over the desk, takes my arm and, with his
stale onion breath—he gobbles an onion even with his coffee,
mister, I'm sure of it—so, he whispered to me that he can't
sleep at all, not even with sleeping pills. Apparently, after his
wife falls asleep, he gets out of bed, and sneaks into the dining
room, barefoot so that she won't hear. He takes all the knick-
knacks off the television—a ballerina, a swan, a toreador, that
sort of thing—and puts in their place a small, gray child's
skull, which he found there, in the pit, and which he keeps hidden in the balcony during the day. He says he keeps it in a bag,
behind the jars of pickles, so that no one will stumble across
it. Anyway. At night he sits in front of that little noggin and
gazes for hours at the crack in the brow, a kind of flower with
nine or ten petals. You can even picture it, can't you? He sees
it as a daisy . . ." (He coughs.) "And in the morning, just as it's
starting to get light outside, he takes the skull in his hands, caresses it, feels the eye sockets, the nose hole, the mouth, around
the ears and it seems that gradually, gradually, he understands
everything that . . ." (At this point ABBA interposed with "Lay
All Your Love on Me.") Then: ". . . to say it to my face, that is
to swear it, just like that, like in court, that because of the skel-

etons at the fort he doesn't have time to breathe let alone pay attention to car horns and trumpets, it's really . . ." (A louder cough, followed by "Time Flies" by Vaya con Dios.) The photographer has been absent from the table for a while. He is not in the toilet, but in front of the café. He has taken his dromedary a bag of dehydrated potato chips. When he comes back, he finds the teacher leaning against the wall, having dozed off. Pusha shrugs and carries on rinsing glasses.

There is not necessarily any need for Allah or the Prophet to recall what the photographer's dromedary used to feed on in its native land; it is sufficient that once, after the calf had been weaned from its gaunt mother, someone looked after him and did not let him perish. And since he arrived here, Aladdin has changed his feed to such an extent that it no longer matters how things stood before he was sold and put on the ship. His preferences are now boiled cabbage, apples, and chocolate, but living under the sign of comradeship he will eat anything except those things that constitute the culinary phobias or reserves of his master. So it is that Aladdin, given that Mr. Sasha cannot, for instance, stand the sight of belly broth and avoids pears because they give him a rash, has never tasted the former creamy-yellow liquid or partaken of the latter sweet and juicy fruit. Aladdin not only accepts beef or chicken soup from the photographer's hands and slurps them with pleasure, he not only gobbles mutton pastrami and fishcakes (eliminating both the one and the other by the complicated process of rumination), but at Easter he also eats (unpeeled) painted eggs and, at Christmas, the traditional pork crackling, sausage, and black pudding. "Even for an animal, particularly a *Camelus drome-*

darius," as Mr. Sasha often asks, over a beer or a coffee, "isn't that proof of apostasy?"

The two met at the Sunday Market, on the outskirts of Brashov, where the photographer, wearing his tinted glasses, a mechanic at his side, was examining the foreign motors. He did not find anything worth buying. There was a gray four-door Opel Kadett, six hundred cc., but the price was a bit steep given the amount of oil it was leaking from its gaskets. There was also a tidy white Fiat Punto, but the steering was iffy and an axle head rattled. Wandering around that ants' nest, Mr. Sasha grew tired of looking at engines and chassis, of questioning and listening, of haggling and asking advice in whispers or signs from his companion, of being elbowed in the crowd and rubbing up against all kinds of strangers, of guarding his pockets. And so he headed off toward the edge of the flea market, where, under a makeshift canopy, they were selling drinks. He had briskly quenched his thirst and lit a cigarette, when he observed not far off, over the tarpaulin of a truck, the peak of a hump and a coffee-colored, elongated head, at the extremity of which the lips and nose were snorting, baring huge teeth. Aladdin was still a calf. When the photographer approached, it lifted its tail and ejected a blackish pat of dung, which it straightaway trampled with all four hoofs. "What great luck!" said Mr. Sasha and, in spite of the mechanic's protests, counted out six hundred dollars and slapped them in the palm of the tall fellow in front of him. (The latter was an electrician who had returned from Jordan a few weeks earlier. He had bought the animal for next to nothing in a bazaar. He had not had it slaughtered, but rather racked himself transporting it two thousand one hundred and twenty-five miles, by sea and land, to his village high in the Rucăr Valley.) On the way home, in a pickup truck, the photographer kept looking through the back window of the cab and discovered that on the dromedary's throat there were eight white points, as big as peanuts, which traced an almost perfect octagon.

Aladdin's life can be divided into two major periods, whose line of separation was not traced according to geographical criteria (the passage from one continent and one climate to another), nor by the power of religions (the abandonment of Islam for the Christian world), nor by the habits of the stomach (the step from vegetal fundamentalism to meat), nor by the lapse of days, months, and years (the transformation of childhood into maturity). For Aladdin, the thread was snapped due to a brown heifer coming into her first heat, for whom he demolished the timber fence of a farmyard, whom he chased through a beech and spruce wood, pummeled, caressed, and ushered into a rocky cleft, full of nettles. He touched her moist, warm muzzle with his rough tongue, butted her back legs with his forehead, and then mounted her after having made clear the meaning of a young camel's will and lust. The dromedary, in order not to be mutilated or poisoned by one of the all too many owners of cattle thereabouts (folk who did not desire any hump-backed cows or camels with horns and udders in their farmyards), with the resigned accord of the photographer, was eventually left without testicles.

Until the day when, by chance, within the perimeter of the fort, not coins and pitchers, not swords, daggers, and arrowheads, not helmets and armor, not statuettes, not temple vases but bones came to light, thousands of bones from who knows how many bodies all buried together, Aladdin had been a familiar sight at the ruins. Mr. Sasha used to frequent the fort more often than the park, cable car station, or waterfall, and his ledger of receipts and payments, a fundamental tome for any freelance professional, clearly showed that those desirous of photos were more numerous among the ruins than anywhere else. The dromedary used to graze contentedly near the stone walls, many of them crumbling and covered in moss and yellowed grasses. He would receive all kinds of things from visitors: sweets, candy floss, wafer biscuits, cookies, chewing gum, chocolate, fruit. They would sometimes even offer him cigarettes, and he would munch them with pleasure, especially the mentholated ones. The photographer used to interpose only in a single case, when Aladdin was enticed with beer, wine, or spirits. Alcohol made him ill (and Mr. Sasha knew this very well), not according to the pattern of indigestion, dizziness, or headaches, rather it was as though that sense of which the veterinarian's scalpel had dispossessed him was impetuously reawakened, and without any particular target. What it was possible to see in such situations was remarkable, testimony to which is provided by photographs in which the dromedary seems to have five legs. But what used to take place was also terrifying, so harebrained was his flight and so unusual were his roars. As a rule, however, Aladdin displayed gentleness. And countless were those—day or weekend trippers, people on vacation, passing foreigners—who wished to immortalize themselves, their faces, garments, and euphoria, on the Arabian carpet draped between the dromedary's neck and hump. Somewhat fearfully they would climb up the little aluminum ladder, then the stepladder was put to one side and they would smile into Mr. Sasha's camera, knowing full well that when the Polaroid picture took on contours and colors, the ramparts and mountains would appear. When discussions about price arose, or quite simply as an exercise in fantasy, Mr. Sasha used to relate something about a fictive Roman legion, made up entirely of camel-riding Egyptians, who had been sent to subdue these lands. For unbelieving interlocutors, the photographer would make reference to Anthony and Cleopatra.

The locals very rarely had their photographs taken on Aladdin's back. They used to do so reservedly and only if the picture was intended for some faraway relative or friend, certainly not for the family album. The dromedary had only represented something out of the usual for at most a week after his appearance in the town. They had all flocked to see him. They had gossiped aplenty and everywhere about Mr. Sasha's decision to buy him, after which they had definitively relegated him to that category of things and creatures that warranted only contempt. For a short time, there had been discussion about him, after the episode with the heifer, but that did not mean that his exoticism had been revived. Lately, the same thing had happened with the Bolivian musicians who played in front of the Carmen Hotel. For three or four days, countless scrutinizing eyes had gazed on the floral shirts and llama-skin Andean headgear, the embroidered bands and scarves, the panpipes, flutes, and tambourines, the olive-skinned faces, and the black, bushy mustaches, while just as many pricked-up ears had listened to those bizarre melodies. "They're just sunburned Gypsies!" the cinema cashier had shouted one afternoon and mockingly laughed out loud, enough to provoke other laughs, whistles, and stupid remarks around her. Luckily for the five mariachi (as well as Aladdin and the photographer, for that matter), the place was full of tourists.

In that small mountain town, they were all waiting for a

team of Argentineans, examples of that rare species of researcher who appeared in the mid-1980s, following four military juntas, in order to provide those killed with an identity and their families with a body for burial.

→>-<+

Lunch at Chez Matilda: the magistrate colonel crumbles slices of bread into his beef broth; the eyes of one of the young prosecutors, the captain, are watering from the chili pepper; confronted with a grilled trout, the other, the lieutenant major, is having a hard time with his knife and fork; the lieutenant of the gendarmes, not at all in his element, keeps sneezing and wiping his nose on the establishment's napkins, which he then stuffs in his pocket. The restaurant differs from an officer's mess. On the walls there are charcoal drawings and watercolors, which depict a lady from the inter-war period, probably the grandmother or aunt of the patroness, Matilda. On the tables there are small faux gas lamps. In one corner there is a fireplace, currently unlit, with a canopy above the hearth.

From the door to the kitchen, from behind a green velour curtain, the waitress hears the discussion, recognizes the voices. She knows that the nasty old man slurping his soup and waiting for a serving of chicken livers has contradicted the one eating fish, saying that the chief of police is not an idiot, but a sly dog who is playing his card. What card, Colonel, sir? He's certifiably stupid, the bald one with the meatballs and chili pepper interrupts. But then the old codger explains that Maxim (she had realized from the very start whom they were talking about) is about to be removed from his post and that is why he is clinging by his teeth to the mass grave, so that he will look like a hero and not get the sack. The hapless lieutenant (she knows the officer of gendarmes from around town) has a stinking cold and only opens his mouth to ask for the salt and some bread. The one eating trout, who skipped the first course, but has ordered two desserts, curd pancakes and glazed apples, says that sly tricks have to be answered with sly tricks and proposes that the major should be guaranteed his post as chief of local police, if he gives up his harebrained stories, which have been driving everyone out of their minds. In the end, sipping a dry red wine, he says that the chief inspectors ought to deal with him as they thought fit.

The waitress comes in with the other dishes (the chicken livers, pork and beans, some sausages with stewed cabbage, and the curd pancakes) and snags her black stocking on the corner of a chair. Oh, how silly! And look at the skin where the threads have burst, as white as cheese! The four officers, three in civvies and one in uniform, look at her. The girl smiles and thinks about how that evening, when she meets him, Maxim will give her money for five new pairs of stockings, not just one.

⤚⤙

The coroner leans down and picks up a scrap of paper from the grass. It is red and wet. He examines it on one side and the other. It must be a candy wrapper. He throws it away.

"Is it true that they kept you there on your knees, wearing nothing but your shirt?" he asks Major Maxim.

"What?" gasps the other.

"There was a frost, wasn't there? Or, I mean, it was very cold. Anyhow, to stay there in your shirt that length of time, bareheaded . . ."

"No . . . Where . . ."

"I'm talking about the police station steps. What are they made of? Stone? Tile? What's there? There must have been snow. Or ice. An hour, an hour and a half sitting already means rheumatism. Or a kidney complaint."

"I didn't . . . You . . ."

"Calm down, Major! Are you trembling? Your face has turned white . . ."

"Look, what do you want?"

"Really, there's no problem at all. So many years have passed, you would fall ill on the spot if it happened again, but now there's no risk, it's all in order. Or from the punches, from the kicks . . . If there hadn't appeared symptoms of . . ."

"How dare you?!" wheezes Maxim. (He does not shout because nearby, twenty-five, thirty, forty feet away, no one has a tape measure to gauge exactly, but in any case nearby, there are many familiar persons: two prosecutors, soldiers, a few journalists, a former political prisoner, and one of the archaeologists.)

"I'm not talking about fractures or internal hemorrhaging, that would have become visible quickly, it would have been apparent. However, there is a risk, from all those blows, of a blood clot appearing, you know how it is, matters relating to neurosurgery, it's more delicate."

"Out with it already! What are you implying?" the chief of police lets fly through his teeth and plants himself right in front of the coroner, his legs apart, hands on his hips.

"What luck, eh? After so many shocks! Thermal, mechanical, perhaps emotional too. I mean—I believe it is possible that there was also an emotional shock. It's not easy to be a policeman and to be made to walk around on all fours, pulled by the necktie, and taken outside like a puppy to pee . . . It's unpleasant, eh! And who would do such a thing to you? A bunch of louts, because there's a revolution . . . No, it's unpleasant! I saw that fellow, the one with the white Mercedes, isn't it him? The one in flip-flops and a vest?"

(The major's eyes have become small, burning. The color of his cheeks is cherry red.)

"You have a healthy body. You eat onions, a lot of onions, isn't that right? I can tell. Maybe the onions helped you, you never know . . . But in the future use mouthwash, whatever flavor you like—it doesn't hurt! I prefer jasmine myself."

"You fag-got! You fag-got!"

Seen from above, let us say from the thick wall at the gate of the fort (a place from which the Roman sentries had also once watched), the scene appeared thus: two men, one broad-shouldered, dressed in a beige suit, the other burly, with a mustache, wearing a police uniform, are walking leisurely by the mass grave, past the people preoccupied with the bones. At one point they stop, the policemen steps in front of the other to tell him something confidential or not quite suitable to be uttered aloud, perhaps a dirty joke. The man in the beige suit laughs heartily, his whole body is shaking with laughter. Then, the officer must have remembered about some meeting or other important business, because he departs in great haste.

→>-<+

Sometimes, without it having any connection to the "I. F. Kissling, Ploesci, Photo-Globe" crest, I felt a kind of pity for the newlywed Paulina, that young bride lost in veils and lace, with the glassy eyes of a cuddly toy, with exaggeratedly long eyelashes (here, in contrast to the bloom of the cheeks and the curve of the lips, the hand that did the retouching had not stayed the brush in time), with an acute misunderstanding of the situation and of the future visible on her face, who had gone so far as to press her temple to the shoulder of the man who had just become her husband (a plump, bald fellow, with a pomaded mustache, satisfied not only with the circumstances, but with life in general: an avuncular type, in fact, not at all a slim gentleman, as Auntie Paulina called the man who had lately been monopolizing her dreams). There they were, against a studio background intended to conjure up the joy of the moment and future happiness (a blossoming or perhaps freshly snow-dusted orchard), framed by a gray passe-partout, as they were then, and before whom Auntie Paulina now says with a sigh, whether I am in the room or not, "What times they were, dear, what times!" omitting to mention the name of Jorgu, uttering it only very rarely. "Ah, the poor deceased." But her nuptial photograph—this was what astonished me, hence also my compassion—did not succeed in dominating the white wall even in the fresh light of the mornings, nor later, toward afternoon, when the sun came level with the window, nor even at the onset of dusk, when the ceiling light or the lamp would be lit. There was something impressive in that object, an irremediable inability to become conspicuous, although it had been and continued to be offered chances to shine. On that expanse of whitewashed wall, there, right in front of my bed, what ruled were the shadows of the foliage, of the curtains billowed by the wind, of the blackbirds, chaffinches, and jays, those of the books and flacons of medicaments on the nightstand. With clean cloths and medicinal spirits, with religiosity and perseverance, Auntie Paulina always made sure that there was not so much as a speck of dust on the gilt frame or the pane of glass that protected her bridal photograph, but she was incapable of giving life to the waxen faces. Reading, idling, as I munched toast, drank marjoram tea, and gulped antacid pills, on waking and on going to bed, I would see only ashen outlines. Fixed or undulating, vague or pregnant, idle or lively, before me filed forms and beings with a terribly short lifespan, shadows the same as all shadows: fascinating, elliptical, courteous. It was a problem of perception. Perhaps my ulcer affected not only my digestion but also my senses. Anyway, it would have been high-handed to break Auntie Paulina's heart, to stop her crooning as her nostalgia welled up. "Listen to what it says on the back," she once called out to me, when I wasn't even in my room, but in the bathroom, with the door open, getting ready to shave. "'Photographic plates are kept for subsequent orders, which can be executed even many years later.'" And when I turned around, she was sitting on the edge of a chair with her head bowed, the photograph in her lap. She was laughing differently from the way she usually did. She was laughing guardedly, but nonetheless I observed the gleam of tears.

"Your problem, darling," she proclaimed one chilly Wednesday, "is that you don't drink coffee because of your diet, and that prevents you from knowing your future." We were on the veranda, in the wicker rocking chairs. There were no cakes on that occasion. I had been dejected to discover in the newspaper—I think I was even gnawing my fingernails—that an important writer was also treating the question of the bones at the Roman fort in a grandiose manner, and Auntie Paulina was studying, using a magnifying glass, one that was not at all small, the lines of the coffee grounds in her cup. "At my age I no longer have any inclination to travel, or even go shopping, but look at this! I can expect a long, very long journey, maybe abroad, because this little boat here is cutting the waves much too impetuously." The poor writer, overcome like so many others by the mass grave, convinced that the new regime was concealing murders committed by the old, could not even imagine that he was abetting the cause of an imbecilic policeman. Something remained murky, a slightly crooked little heart, a peevish dog, and a clown surrounded the boat, as though they wanted to jump on board or accompany its glide through the waters. Someone had a mind to batten on to Auntie, to invite himself on the journey or profit from it. "Hmm, not even here do they leave me in peace! At least if it were someone bearable, a bit of company doesn't do any harm." However, the destination could by no means be clearly descried. Perhaps a tiny little shape might have resembled a letter *O*, but Auntie Paulina categorically refused to go to "'Olland." "I have tulips in my own backyard, dear, a whole host of yellow and red ones. So what if I don't have any purple ones? I don't need them! I'm not keen on windmills and then again you can see clearly that it's a small *o*, God knows, it's not a capital." As I was peeling my boiled egg, my four o'clock egg, I thought that it would be good to send the novelist a letter, not so much to enlighten him, to explain how I, as an archaeologist, thought things stood, as to save him from solidarity with the militiaman. "I haven't confessed to you until now that I get seasick." (She fidgets in her chair, vaguely blushing.) "I have been in a boat just once in my life, at Slănic, on my honeymoon. Jorgu's sister was there with her little girls. Those little scorpions kept splashing me and grimacing. I felt as though I were about to give up the ghost." The boat must be a symbol, nothing more. It could not be anything else. She could not even conceive of traveling by water. "Dear, if it is a question of a cruise, I give up the idea from the very start. I'm better off at home, with my pots and pans, with my chickens, than on the most luxurious liner in the world. What a frightful country that 'Olland is too, nothing but canals everywhere, nothing but water. I think only Venice could be more dreadful!" In the dry coffee grounds it could unmistakably also be read that some money was going to arrive: a tidy sum, not a trifle. But questions kept cropping up: could it be that measly pension? ("Ah, no, I don't think so, the fact that the postman is on his way has never come up in my coffee grounds.") A present? ("Ha, ha, ha, a person that courteous has yet to be born.") Could it be a legacy? ("Phooey, what nonsense.") A prize in some competition? ("Darling, you know me: have you ever seen me playing the lottery or bingo? Have you ever seen me cutting out tokens from boxes of laundry soap or collecting beer-bottle tops?") Might it be the rent? ("Well now, that's the limit, I mean, here you are sitting two feet away from me and not a word about paying and you leave it to come up in my fortunetelling . . .") There followed a few minutes of silence. Auntie Paulina had set aside the cup and the magnifying glass. She wrapped herself more snugly in her brick-red traveling rug, and peered outside, not toward the motionless clouds, nor toward the cluster of beeches across the road. Perhaps she was gazing into space.

On the subject of fortunes, Mrs. Eugenia, Jenny, her neighbor, had once been a rich woman, her past was illustrious, but when she had left her old house to move here, she took with her no fewer than fifty-two ordinary cats ("European, not mongrels, you hear . . ."), which, during transport, she had striven to shut inside a cage ordered specially, but on the way they had escaped in every direction when one of the moving men loosened some of the bars. They had mewled dreadfully until their release, it was something unimaginable, people were gawping as though at a fairground, then the cats had leapt maddened from the van, which was moving at full speed, and vanished who knows where—yards, roofs, ditches, most of them into the woods. Their owner whacked two or three of the porters with her umbrella, refused to pay the one who had facilitated the escape, left her entire goods and chattels in the hands of a frail niece, a schoolgirl with acne, and, livid, trembling, she had set off in search of the cats along the streets traveled by the van. For almost a week, from early in the morning until nightfall, she traced and retraced the two- or three-mile route ("you should have seen her, Lord, Lord, with a thin shawl over her shoulders, hunched over the way she is, with her little steps, leaning on her walking stick, all the while shouting, 'Come on, girls! Come on, boys! Come to mama, kitties!' She had no more voice left, dear. She had become completely hoarse. 'Celia! Rosy, Lenny, Puffa, come to mama!' The children would tease her and stick to her like burrs, there would be some drunk or other whistling at her"), she managed to recover only eleven cats and, after a cold October shower, to contract pneumonia. As far as Auntie Paulina was concerned, between the idea that a cat in the lap regulates the heart rate and the idea that cat hair causes hydatidic cysts, she preferred the latter.

"You must, deary, take care of your health otherwise than with toast and fistfuls of pills," she said to me later. My insufferable ulcer would be vanquished or, in any case, soothed, if I were to abide by her advice, because she had discovered the key, the secret, the cure, without any need for guiding dreams or masses for salvation. The therapy was simple. I had merely to knock on the door of Mrs. Embury ("Dear Eugenia!") and obediently listen as she laid out the jacks, queens, and kings ("She reads the cards magnificently, so that you too will find out, my boy, what is to become of the problem that is weighing on your heart, with those skeletons at the fort"). She was convinced that, after a visit to Jenny or, perhaps after two or three, I would find tranquility and, even if I didn't forgive the chief of police, at least I would no longer wish to flatten his nose. "Your nerves are on tintacks, why don't you get it into your head once and for all that they're at the root of it, not your stomach. Don't keep swallowing all those pills, what you need is to know something for certain, never mind what, all this agitation is killing you . . ." The resolution of the events at the archaeological site, one that I desired as hastily as possible and, at least out of professional honesty, if not for other motives, as justly as possible, would be deciphered in Mrs. Embury's tired pack of playing cards, almost a sacred object, which was never absent from the table in her day room. The fact that I did not believe in that theory counted very little. But my look or the position of my body or something else entirely betrayed my skepticism and Auntie Paulina threatened that I would never see pies or dumpling soup again, forever and ever. And she suggested to me that I should not forget the old folk of the town. ("Only avoid Paraschiva, because all you'll get from her are tales about monks and recipes for monastic fasts") and (who knows why?) it was only now that she concluded the story about Slănic and her honeymoon. The young Paulina, not lost in veils and lace like the one in the photograph, but wearing a tight-fitting, orange summer dress, had not sufficiently resisted the rocking of the boat and nor had she been able to put up endlessly with the jokes of her nieces. And she had vomited.

How niggling Auntie Paulina's silences were! She sighed more heavily than usual, with a whistling noise. She would raise her chin peevishly and gaze at the ceiling whenever I was in the vicinity. She cooked only my favorite dishes, which she would then share out, while they were still piping hot, to the neighbors and stray dogs. There was no other way out of it, and so, after plenty of postponements, I was obliged, one rainy day, a Thursday to be precise, to visit Eugenia Embury. I knocked on the door loudly and for a long while. I even tapped on one of the windows, not necessarily because I wanted to be let in, but in order to spare Paulina from the fit of indignation she would have had if I had explained to her that the doorbell was broken and her friend had not heard my decorous tapping. I was greeted by a girl with tousled hair, whom I had certainly woken from slumber: Mrs. Embury's niece, who, so many years after the fifty-two cats had escaped from the van, no longer had pimples and no longer seemed at all frail. Her nightgown was no more than a shirt, but not some linen kept from childhood, small and frayed. It was satin lingerie. She returned my greeting sleepily and, heading toward the dining room to announce me to her aunt, she bent down and leisurely stroked a tomcat. She had a bottom like a strawberry.

The playing cards were spread over the table in all kinds of rows and decks, some face up, others face down. I could not make anything of the way they were divided up. Steam rose from the teacups. Auntie Jenny's whitish-purple, blotched hands were trembling slowly, and her voice blurred with that of a legal expert on the radio. Employers are required to communicate on a quarterly basis to the county labor office . . . somebody of diamonds, a man, is speaking ill of you to friends or relatives, he knows you are far away and that you can't defend yourself, he has a vested interest, he is not doing so for nothing . . . point b, paragraph three, expressly stipulates that . . . we need to throw light on this intrigue, because, look, some women and a young man, yes, a young man, the knave of hearts keeps coming up, hmm! Hmm! And they are well intentioned, they want to hold counsel and to make an important decision . . . by submitting an application to the local authorities . . . five hearts in a row, the knave and another four, the knave keeps coming up, you see? It's something to do with a house. The young man might play the game of the man of diamonds and try to turn the women against you. The legal expert was bidding farewell to the listeners as I finished my second sweet cheese pie and learned that I was going to have to deal with an illness for a short while, probably a cold. As for the matter of the house, things had been clarified earlier: taking advantage of the credulity of the young man of hearts and his influence over the group of women, the man of diamonds was seeking by any means to prevent me from starting on the building work. For me, the outcome was predictable, but I did not tell the old lady anything. I did not breathe a word. The man of diamonds was going to succeed, because I was not in the least bit concerned with real estate projects. The girl's slippers were linen clogs with quite a high heel. When she leaned against the table to pick a few raisins out of the pie, she bent her left leg sharply, as though running. Her heel looked like an apple.

"What's with these manners, you?" Auntie Jenny snapped. She shielded the plate with one of her palms and shook her bamboo stick threateningly in the air. Then she introduced us. After she uttered my full name, with my father's initial and all three forenames, her head began to shake, with her eyes wide, huge, her mouth twisted, and a tear or two trickling down one cheek. She did not make a sound, except for something like a muffled sob every now and then. At first I was frightened, but it turned out not to be a heart attack or anything else bad. That was simply the way Mrs. Embury laughed. She told us that I should introduce myself as an archimandrite instead of an archaeologist. The girl, her granddaughter, was called Josephina, and, by the family, Jojo. Jojo went off into another room to study for her exams, without much enthusiasm, as if she had been sent to chop wood. Behind her, the old lady rapped on the floor with her walking stick, after which, now sprightly, she set about shuffling the cards once again. It was only fair to explain to her how things really stood, which is to say, why I had come to visit her and, above all, what it was that had been grating on my nerves for a good few weeks. And I told her, spluttering at first, in a roundabout way, then as frankly as could be, that I did not believe in fortunetelling one bit, nor in that business with the coffee grounds, nor in reading the cards, nor in cowry shells—in none of it. I told her that the only reason I had come was to appease Auntie Paulina. I was afraid she might fly into a rage and send me packing, but her head was again seized by that comical shaking, and the sobs reemerged from between her translucent lips. She was laughing. This time with many more tears, streaming down both cheeks. After she calmed down, she pushed the teacups and the cake to one corner of the table, gave me a wink (oho, how many wrinkles furrowed her eyelids!), rose with difficulty from her chair, and, with short steps, headed for the sideboard by the window. She returned with a bottle of brandy and two greenish stemmed glasses. We clinked glasses, she kissed me on the forehead, and declared that she had always been crazy about men who didn't go in for mumbo-jumbo.

At some point, soon after Eugenia Embury's grandfather clock had struck three, I thought how welcome it would be if in school textbooks there were an imaginative exercise, an inverse composition: reduce the following description to a single idea: ". . . to drink brandy while you chat with a lovely person, to sink among the soft and cozy cushions of an armchair, to run your fingers through the fur of a cat (and there, you had one within reach wherever you sat down), to take a sip of that mahogany liquid (in such a text, it would be unpardonable for *ruddy-brown* to appear), to let it pinch the tongue and palatal arch for a while (how inexpressive *roof of the mouth* would have sounded!), to allow it to diffuse its aromas and only then to abandon it to the long and sinuous digestive tract (nor would the verb *to swallow* have had any place), and after that, to say

wholeheartedly that the chief of police is a bandit and a clod-
hopper, to say all kinds of things that one cannot usually say,
not as one does in confession, but in a light, relaxed way, just to
say them, and to have that lovely person gaze at you with fond-
ness and solidarity." Doing such an exercise, I for one would
have unreservedly answered that it was a question of joy. Perhaps even of a rare joy. However, to make a concession to all
those schoolchildren who, faced with such an assignment for
homework, would have summed up the experience as an example of idleness, the influence of alcohol, an insult to the forces
of law and order, gerontophilia, or who knows what, I would
also settle for "voluptuousness." God knows, all I did was to
recount during one afternoon how the archaeological dig at the
Roman fort had been stopped, how much bitterness springs up
when you search people's eyes, and how that bitterness accu-
mulates in the heart, in the lungs, and in the stomach like a per-
fidious gas, capable of spontaneously combusting. I described,
for instance, the tiny pupils of Mr. Titus Maeriu, drowned in
their milky blue irises and a tortured past, smoldering like em-
bers whenever the origin and age of the mass grave was put
in doubt. A smoldering maintained by over-zealous care, by
the fear that the suffering of his comrades might be profaned.
He was like those war invalids who are unable to conceive that
others might be left infirm because of an untreated fingernail
infection or an accident in a locksmith's workshop. Mr. Maeriu,
who had had to endure interrogations and prison, who knew
like no other how far the vileness of Party henchmen had gone,
would not for the life of him believe that the grave was not a
case of political crime. For all his current labels — retired engineer, author of a doctoral thesis on the resistance of tunnels

in sedimentary rock, father, grandfather, and, above all, great-grandfather—he seemed convinced that all the mass graves in the world were the consequence of summary executions perpetrated by the Communists. "The poor man," said Eugenia, "he is bitterly deceiving himself and yet he is so right!" "Isn't it sad, madam, isn't it sad?" I replied. As I was chewing the last sweet-cheese-and-raisin pie, slowly, as the doctor ordered, I realized that brandy, starting not quite with the first glass, but later, predisposes one to philosophizing. "Mr. Petrus, one can fool oneself while being so much in the right," she said and invited me to lunch—it was already approaching four o'clock. Shortly before the dumpling soup, Jojo arrived, bringing with her the somnolence and unease of a student on the threshold of exams. She was wearing a sleeveless housecoat made of blue Indian silk.

After the greenish stemmed glasses had been refilled, I discovered that Auntie Jenny was a Lady. When she was just seventeen and getting ready to finish her studies at the Notre-Dame Pension, not in Paris, but in Ploieşti, she, Eugenia, had fallen passionately in love with the young Lord Neil Embury, the representative of a British company at the city's refineries. She had lived a whirlwind and incandescent romance with him and, with the blessing of an Anglican priest brought specially by airplane from Salonica, she had become his wife on the very day that Chamberlain, who was suffering a bout of the flu, found the strength, divine as he initially believed, undoubtedly diabolical, as he realized not long afterward, not to condemn by official communiqué, or even by letter at the embassy level, the extensive troop deployments in the demilitarized Rhineland zone. Neil, thirty-one years old at the time, was the possessor of curly blond sideburns, an alabaster lorgnette, gray eyes (quote: "like the heavens before snowfall"), an exquisite collection of cravats, and an honest laugh (further quote: "Do you know what it means to laugh freely? Freely, freely . . . that is, not to care whether it is becoming or not . . ."). She met him at Number 34, Princess Elena Street, the house of the eldest of the Ionescu brothers, the owners of the Podu-Fetii estate and the refractory-brick works at Pleaşa. The occasion was a muted Easter holiday dinner. She had come there with her father, the lawyer of the hosts, of the "Brotherhood Unlimited Company," to be more accurate, and it chanced that she choked on a fishbone from a baked Danube mackerel. There was panic, she could not breathe, she clutched her throat with both hands, one of the guests shouted for salts, a gentleman strove to prise open her lips and get her to swallow some bread, another endlessly repeated, like a cracked gramophone record, "Breathe deeply! Breathe deeply!" Someone, a woman, had the idea of sprinkling her face with wine, a rather sweet pinot blanc, and at last, from somewhere behind, there came an unexpected blow of a palm, light, though precise, not at all painful, but efficient and lifesaving. The company had not yet come to their senses, they were still swarming frightened and impotent around her, but Lord Embury, he who had applied that providential blow to her nape, was laughing his heart out, a laugh that was loud and free, do you understand, a laugh that was free. She had felt extremely embarrassed. For the rest of the evening she had not raised her eyes from her plate, and it was as if her forehead, temples, and cheeks were burning. Somewhere above her ankles, she was being pricked by a needle. She imagined, she actually saw a running sewing machine, on whose pedal an unknown foot pressed from time to time, a leg clothed in the soft fabric of a man's trousers, the color of oil, and shod with an elegant boot, of the same coal-black. Before leaving, urged on insistently by the industrialist Ionescu, the eldest of the homonymous brothers, and with less enthusiasm by her father, she had made her way over to Neil Embury and thanked him. Touching her shoulder with his ring finger, the oilman, with comical pronunciation and abstract grammar, had said something about Dickens and an enchanted fishbone and had promised to visit her at the pension, in order to convince her that the effects of his slap had been nothing but salutary. The visit might have been short or conventional, or might not have occurred at all, but things were to be otherwise. In the upper-floor dormitory, beneath the rafters, more than an hour after the announcement of lights-out, when most of the girls were sleeping and only a few were still fidgeting between starched sheets into which had lately seeped the odor of spring, a soft tap was heard against the window. She, Eugenia, pulled her blanket over her face and in the perfect darkness she saw once more a sewing machine being pedaled by an elegant black boot, pricking her above the ankles with its relentless needle. Tumult erupted in the dormitory. The tap repeated itself, calmly, evenly. Against the luminous background of the window could be made out an arm descending from the eaves. The swift steps of the mother-pedagogue pattered down the corridor, the door opened, then the window, the mother-pedagogue herself opened the window, and from above, from the roof, there appeared a man's face, upside-down, with forehead pointing to the ground and chin to the sky, framed by prominent cheekbones, accompanied by a merry and powerful laugh. The mother-pedagogue turned into a statue, eleven pupils of the Notre-Dame Pension of Ploieşti screamed, gasped, pouted, trembled, groaned, giggled, and so on, while the twelfth in that dormitory, she, Eugenia, calmly approached the window, stepped with bare and rosy feet onto the sill, grasped the hands that stretched down to her and allowed herself to be lifted up to the roof, onto the enameled tiles, which had a greenish gleam on sunny days. "I thought there had to be something behind the tint of these glasses," I said to Auntie Jenny.

The marriage was not officiated in front of an altar, although Neil had tried to stage something at the Cişmeaua Mavrogheni Church, but in the end he had not managed to persuade the parish priest that the service should be conducted to the accompaniment of a boogie-woogie band, with real Negroes, and conclude with congratulations of "God bless you." And so the religious ceremony had taken place by a peasant wayside cross, up which climbed a few shoots of celandine, almost as far as the words graven in Cyrillic script on the stone. Neither Eugenia, who was wearing a pink dress and a flowery-white hat without a veil, nor Lord Embury, dressed in a summer suit the color of a duck egg, nor the pallid and reticent Anglican priest, badly shaken by the airplane that had brought him from Salonica and then by the automobile that had transported him across the plain, through wheat fields and young tobacco plantations, nor the two witnesses, third-rate actors picked up in a Bucharest café for a substantial fee, could decipher anything of the Slavonic text, except for the year 1851. Neil had chosen the spot because it belonged to the category of things or events, few in number, that could cause him to exclaim *Wonderful!* He had once ascertained, during a quail shoot, that, by climbing on the small cross, only three feet in height, you could cast your gaze beyond the drab line of the horizon, contoured exclusively by cereal crops, and see the expanse of the lake and woods at Căldăruşani. Immediately after he had slipped the ring onto her finger, he took Eugenia by the waist, lifted her like a baby onto the top of the cross, and let her make the incomparable visual leap for herself. Eugenia's eyes were met with a sea of light. The lake was imbued with all the strength of the noonday sun. Lord Embury, indifferent to the fury that had overcome the priest (more and more purple-faced, the latter had turned his back on the bride and groom, muttering something, probably a prayer, and clenching the Gospels between his fingers), treating the two ham actors as though they were not there (one of them kept yawning and, with the tip of his shoe, was slowly flattening an ant's nest, while the other, with the aid of a bit of straw, was fastidiously cleaning the dirt from beneath his fingernails), began by kissing the buckle of her white sandals, then the patches of rosy skin between the straps. He moved up to the ankles, repeatedly circled them with his lips, engulfed their roundness a few times, kissed his way up her calves, up to her knees and thighs, sometimes descending but quickly returning, and went ever higher, until his head was completely lost under the hem of her pink dress, remaining there for quite a while.

It is highly likely that Auntie Jenny would not have related the wedding episode to me in such detail, but, in the armchair in her living room, I reached the conclusion that, just as ulcers are the foe of conversation, so brandy is the ally of imagination, probably one of its trustiest friends. What is certain is that, once his daughter was wed, the lawyer of the "Brotherhood Unlimited Company," a person of innate pragmatism, was able to dispel his boundless fury and put a stop to all the retaliatory actions he had launched against the English oilman before he became his son-in-law. With a huge sponge, he wiped away almost all the black moments of the near past: the kidnapping of Eugenia from the respectable Notre-Dame Pension in Ploieşti, the five-week elopement, the contradictory and wholly insupportable rumors about the life of the lovers (one lady, the wife of Magistrate G., had seen them bathing stark naked in the lake at Cernica Monastery during the holiest moment of the liturgy; a high-ranking officer of the gendarmes maintained that, on repeated occasions and sundry highways, he had failed to stop the red Duessenberg Straight speedster, eight aligned cylinders, 4,900 cc., and 265 horsepower, which, with Neil at the wheel and Eugenia beside him, would sometimes be doing over a hundred miles an hour; a refined lady, who happened to be the lawyer's mistress, related how she had heard that the lord had lost a fabulous sum at the casino in Constantia, after which, with Eugenia riding piggy-back, a bottle of champagne in his hand, he traversed the sea wall from one end to the other, neighing like a stallion; the administrator of the Vega refinery complained that a large pile of invoices had accumulated on his desk, which the Englishman was late in paying, while in reply to the letter the lawyer had sent Lord Embury he had received a postcard from Vienna, showing none other than the happy couple in front of the Prater Palace; in the end, Mother Theodosia herself, the headmistress of the Notre-Dame Pension in Ploieşti, unable to content herself merely with the immediate expulsion of the girl, also paid a call on the lawyer, to demand imperatively that he, in his capacity as father, citizen, and Christian, should put a stop by any means possible to a relationship that had rendered her pupils ill). But as father-in-law of Lord Embury, as opposed to outraged father, the lawyer had become a different man. After rapid, extensive, and costly renovation, he placed his small manor in Valeni at the disposal of the young couple, for Sunday outings and short holidays. He deposited a significant sum in Eugenia's account, borrowed from various moneylenders, so that she might complete her wardrobe in a manner befitting her new status. He gave his son-in-law a race-horse, not a champion, it is true, but a platoon horse, received as a present from a large-pocketed client. All these gestures of goodwill, which were intended to be taken as an expression of paternal affection, but also to serve as a bridge from errant youth to responsible family life, did not, however, produce any echo. The house in Valeni was never on the circuit of the newlyweds, the horse remained in the care of the stable hands at the racetrack, without its new master paying any attention to it or entering it in any of the horse-and-trap derbies, and Eugenia's account, for all its symbolism as a marital trousseau, was never touched, accumulating healthy interest. Neil and Eugenia lived far away, always somewhere else, constantly fueling, by vocation, distance, and eccentricity, the drawing-room discussions of the town. One day, when the lawyer had already been bedridden for a number of months (the mistress had for quite some time redirected her attentions to a perfume salesman; the "Brotherhood Unlimited Company" was already long since legally represented by another wearer of the gown, et cetera, et cetera), he was informed, through the same grapevine, that he was a grandfather. The news instantly removed him from beneath the bedsheets, much to the ire of the attendant doctor, who declared on that occasion that bow tie and brilliantine are not worth a bean in the fight against tuberculosis. Telegraphing the English oilman's address in Bucharest, an address where, as he very well knew, Lord Embury set foot only once in a blue moon, this was the last time that the father tried to pick up the trail of his daughter. In the evening, with a high fever and fits of severe coughing, he returned to his sickbed, submitting more docilely than usual to the compresses applied by the nurse. Three weeks later, the invalid received an unmarked envelope, an envelope that contained a photograph of a sleeping baby surrounded, in his miniature bed, by eight cats. Before studying the baby's features (subsequently, with the aid of a magnifying glass, he was to do so hundreds of times), the lawyer was overwhelmed by a persistent sensation of suffocation, from the imaginary animal hair he could feel wafting all around.

At last, Eugenia appeared in the house of her childhood one warm October day, at around lunchtime. She was accompanied by little Jonathan (whom his first nanny, a woman with respect for breeding and apple pies, was to call Yonatan) and was transporting, in a large wicker trunk, the eight cats. Neil, now redundant in a country with too few highways and golf courses once the refineries had come under direct German control, had set off for London and subsequently his country seat, in order to prepare for the arrival of his one true love and his firstborn son. His departure had been forced, even a race against the clock, and Eugenia, in spite of much pleading and insistence, had refused to accompany him before seeing her dying father at least one more time. And it was here that history intervened, with its perfectly prescheduled agenda, with its clearly marked tracks for each and all. The couple's love, long the unrivalled source of high-society conversation, collective rumor, and feminine envy, was transformed into an insignificant particle, caught up, along with millions of other particles, in chaotic motion. It was not a case of Brownian motion. It was a case of war.

Neil Embury, a lieutenant under the new circumstances, fell in North Africa, a matter discovered only much later. Eugenia Embury, after burying her father not so much as a month after they were reunited, discovered the other side of the coin to being the wife of a lord, firstly in the Prussian version, then the native, then the Russian, and finally the motherland's version once again. There followed house arrest, short periods of imprisonment, opened correspondence, confiscation of property, interrogations, yet more periods of imprisonment, and the transformation of the charming little Jonathan Embury into the adult Ion Emburescu, a lathe operator here, in this small mountain town where a mass grave has been discovered, an alcoholic, which is perhaps why he passed to a better world at the age of not even fifty. Auntie Jenny bred and adored a multitude of cats. She took care of educating her granddaughter Josephina even before the loss of her son. She sought and found moments of peace in gardening and games of patience. She always made a delicious sweet-cheese-and-raisin pie. She was invited annually to the Christmas party at the British embassy, after it reopened: She went on each occasion, ignoring the chicaneries and threats of the authorities, and always came home with small gifts. Such as the brandy.

➤-◄-

And Jojo did not merely have a bottom like a strawberry and heels like apples. She had accumulated numerous and perfumed fruits, some visible, as in a salad with whipped cream and a little rum, others hidden who knows where, as beneath the icing of a cake. On the evening when we set out together toward the fort, after Eugenia Embury's tales and brandy, I was in the mood for all kinds of horticultural comparisons, excepting species from the class of legumes, and she did not attempt to discourage me. For a while she held my arm, since as soon as we left the house it began to rain and we were obliged to shelter under a single umbrella. She did this unselfconsciously. She was very playful: she would shorten her stride, quicken her pace, jump over puddles or circumvent them with arms raised like wings. She imitated the cheeping of the birds or the growling and barking of the dogs we met. She answered raucously a gaggle of geese invigorated by so much water, and she laughed at the spluttering engine of a motorcar, copying its sound with her lips. On the way, I often thought of falling silent. It seemed to me that I was boring her, but she kept on insisting, "Speak! Speak!" And I spoke. It is astonishing how I managed to speak for almost three hours, first as we were walking and then on the veranda of the cabin among the ruins, the archaeologists' house. We spoke of Roman military campaigns and strategies, about life in the isolated garrisons, about the mirage of the imperial capital and about the vices of the soldiers, about ornaments and hygiene, about punishments and rewards, about wine. The fruit bowl before me must have been brimming with varieties, because later I realized that I had not uttered a single word about my obsessions of the moment: the interruption of the archaeological dig and the controversy surrounding the mass grave. Jojo, resting her chin on her palms, listened and gazed at me. What were her eyes? Walnuts? Figs? Long after it had grown dark, she asked me why the Romans, when making war and ruling provinces, did not bring with them easy women from back home, or at least slave girls, so that they would not be forced to cool the ardors of the flesh with strangers and thus give birth to so many peoples. I did not know what to reply. We returned still arm in arm, although it was no longer raining and the umbrella was shut. We arranged our next meeting for fifteen hours later.

CHAPTER THREE

→>-<←

FIRSTLY HE RAISED HIS INDEX finger. And the finger, full of scars, dried like a fish in sun and wind, paused for a few moments in midair, next to his temple, then started jerking, so that it set the brim of his straw hat trembling. Shortly after those gestures (interpreted as purificatory, remindful, chiding, foreboding, forgiving, moralizing, and in a host of other ways), he would utter: *Thrice has the Mother of God descended from the Heavens to show Her succor and faith to Onufrie.* The voice resounded each time in the same way, neither more gladly, nor more gloomily, neither more briskly, nor more drawlingly. He would say it countless times a day—in the morning, when with a tin trumpet he would wake the disciples who were sleeping too sweetly, and then later, as he was preparing the brushes and paints, and when he handed out trowels, hods, and tasks to his assistants, before and after lunch, when he laid his heavy palm in blessing upon the heads of those visitors who did not shirk the poor box, at sunset, when they all stopped work and gathered around a dish of rice, beans, or mushroom stew. He also said it at night, in solitude, before prayers and going to bed, in his hut near the pine with nine crowns and the small chapel at its foot. Then, with his forefinger he would threaten the north wall, because on the left-hand side of the icons and the icon lamps he believed that evil spirits entered.

→>-<←

How many things are in need of explanation! Before anything else, it should be known that since the age of six (an approximate age, because no one can guess the birth date of a child found on a riverbank), since one Sunday in October, when he first went to the fair, he had no longer gone bareheaded. There, he had seen a whirligig; dancing bears with rings in their noses; a woman with tattooed cheeks and belly, a huge snake draped around her neck; a man dressed as a three-headed dragon, ready to breathe flames at any moment; two plump horses, one dappled and with a yellow mane, the other with a gray beard and extraordinarily shaggy from the knees down; large sand-filled sacks of buffalo hide that all the stout young fellows were crowding around to punch; a panther with a muzzle and convict's chains around its legs; all kinds of peddlers, stalls, and tents; a makeshift bowling alley; a tightrope-walking dwarf; a throng of gawpers; a boat hanging from a wooden frame, used as a swing for twenty folk; Gypsies in droves; a curly little dog wearing a frock and whining to the rhythm of an accordion; a number of tables above which playing cards and crumpled banknotes constantly whirled; and, somewhere among all the rest (this he recalled the best, because, accustomed to sleeping in stables, lofts, barns for maize, hencoops, wherever he could, he had been thinking of his own skin), an old man who was selling powders for bedbugs, ticks, fleas, and lice. He had eaten a gingerbread heart and drunk a cup of millet beer, received for free from a peddler woman, but what he chiefly understood from that whole day, although at a fair perhaps the contrary would have served him well, was that no one would laugh at him if he wore something on his head. At dawn, when he was about to set off for the fair with old biddy Vutza, she had stopped in the middle of the yard, muttering, gone into the parlor (not before spitting thrice for having turned back in her way), rummaged in a chest for a time, pulled out a tatty hat, and crammed it over his ears. He never discovered whether she had done so out of pity, as payment because he had lugged for her the sack of walnuts and sugar beets almost eight miles over the fields, or so that he would not bring her shame by reason of his oddity. However it may have been, he took it as a good deed, among the best done to him in his life. As soon as he got back to the village, he began carefully to tend to the hat, without caring that the cloth was shiny with wear; with red thread, the first that came to hand, he patched up the holes made by moths, he reinforced the stitching, he picked off the flecks, and tightened it enough so that it no longer fell over his eyebrows. He did not part with it for eight years, taking it off his head only at night, after making sure that no one was lurking to see his hair. Once in a while, when the hat had become too small, not because it had shrunk (he never washed it, but sometimes it would be wetted by the rain), but because he himself had grown continuously, he used to let out the seam: there was material aplenty, for the deceased had been a big-headed man in every respect. At the same time, he continued to cut the tuft on his crown a number of times a day, hiding himself, seeking a place, no matter where he was or what was happening, where he could shield himself from the prying eyes of others. In the pocket of his trousers he always had the scissors that he has even now, as he builds a monastery in pious honor of the Holy Mother of God, who *thrice descended from the Heavens to show him Her succor and faith,* a pair of scissors that had been old from the very start, and were today very old indeed, received from Father Nae, the one who had nicknamed him Tufty. Again, it is hard to establish whether the scissors were a gift or wages paid to the child, this time for winnowing yellow bean pods, from which he had gleaned, one Wednesday in September 1931, some dozen bushels of clean white beans, ready for the priest's wife to put in the soup. In any case, in the memory and heart of the adult who ripened from that child, it is still a matter of a good deed, another among the best in his life, even if Father Nae had called him Tufty long before receiving him into the church and baptizing him Gherghe, in memory of a brother dead in Turtucaia, as the woman who had picked him up in his swaddling clothes from the bank of the river had wished and who, for at least that much, was worthy of being regarded as his adoptive mother. And Tufty was what they always called him anyway. No one ever called him Gherghe, not even her, the one who had found him, put him on his feet and later, when he was twelve and already looked like a man, had taken him to the house of the Lord so that he would not remain a pagan. However, from the time he acquired the hat from old biddy Vutza until he left the village where all knew his oddity, the nickname came to sound more and more like a man's name and less like a taunt. This was due to a number of occurrences: one evening after the fair, with his shovel-like palms he had broken the lips of one, bruised the nose of another, and bent double the third of the boys who had been following him and snatching that shabby cloth hat from his head. Eight months later, when the doctor's assistant, somewhat tipsy after a wake, had thought to squeeze him in his arms on the main street and throw his hat in the ditch, Tufty had bitten his hand so hard that the assistant had urgently required four stitches. Another

night, one chilly autumn with rains that forgot to end, as if by
a miracle there was a fire that burned one of the haycocks left
in the yard by Nitzica, who had tied Tufty's hat to the lamppost
of the inn and tried to catch him by the tuft and lift him up. Finally, on the very day of his baptism, when he wore a white
shirt for the first time, a shirt that had belonged to the other
Gherghe, the one who had breathed his last at Turtucaia, he
had poked his unusually long forefinger, unscarred at the time,
into the left ear of Auntie Sorica, leaving her half deaf, because
she had been shouting at the top of her voice that the servant
of the Unclean One should not be allowed into the church. After that episode, no one else molested his hat, even if, unseen
by stranger's eye, the tuft beneath, a very thick bunch of hair
two fingers above his brow, grew almost eight inches every
four hours and had to be docked, as it does now.

In that village on the plain whence he departed forever at the
age of about fifteen one sultry and dusty afternoon, when
against the sky, in the absence of clouds, flocks of starlings
were furling and bunching, many stories had circulated regarding his no-longer-to-be-seen tuft. One woman used to say
(as though a newborn babe could have had hair instead of
down) that his true mother had picked him up by that tuft when
she abandoned him on the shingle bank, and that the Good
God, on seeing such a depraved act, had marked the spot. Another, in whom Auntie Sorica must have unswervingly believed, said that no place the Unclean One thrust his tail could
remain untainted and that the poor woman, whoever she was,
knew very well why she was abandoning the child. A version
that did not pass over the fact that Tufty had been found by the

river on the day after the feast of the Prophet Elijah spoke of
the matchless abundance of hair as a bounty of the earth, because he, the newborn babe, had lain there like a pumpkin,
and that tiny as he was he could not sit up or crawl, and so
all the accumulated blessings of the prophet had settled upon
his hair, rather than being distributed among the cucumbers,
tomatoes, wheat, and barley. Old biddy Silca, to whom they
all went, ignoring the doctor's assistant, when they could not
rid themselves of some infirmity, and who extracted good and
evil from herbs, flowers, and roots, reckoned that infusions
of his hair (she assiduously used to seek the tufts he threw
away every four hours, on rare occasions finding one) healed
rheumatism better than anything else, a sign that the tuft did
not grow from the skin, but from the skull, if not from the
brain itself. Father Nae, so often questioned on the subject—
otherwise satisfied not only with how the young lad winnowed
beans but also with how he gathered plums, stacked sacks of
wheat and maize flour, picked potatoes, curried horses, caught
crabs, collected and burnt garbage, trimmed vines, sheared
sheep, and many, many other things—would usually limit himself to observing that the ways of the Lord are mysterious.
One Palm Sunday, constrained by the churchgoing women to
render his opinion (they had cornered him by the church door,
vociferating, gesticulating, constantly straightening their head
scarves, which were slipping down their perspiring brows), he
had turned greenish-white in the face, then scarlet, then
greenish-white again (his face, with its large chops and narrow
forehead, had, for the space of a minute, looked like a huge
duck's egg) and proclaimed the Leper's Kiss as the most important teaching of the Holy Scriptures. Then, to illustrate his

point, the priest had sought out the boy in the throng, taken him in his arms, removed his hat (it was the only time Tufty docilely allowed his head to be uncovered), and fervently kissed the tuft, which was just approaching its maximum length before shearing, eight inches. As bristly as a shaving brush, the hair on his crown gleamed bluish-black in the sun, provoking a collective exclamation of amazement and silencing the women. But the history of that unheard-of tuft, the history, rather than the mythology, in its pure form, untainted by Christian fabulation or by heresy, a form to which all too few had access in the absence of the boy's natural mother, is altogether different. The young Stanca, a maid with a small and rather threadbare dowry—because she was orphaned by her father and had five brothers—otherwise with locks as yellow as honey reaching her waist, good at the ring dance, quick to smile and with sweetly gazing eyes, had become pregnant after a weeklong love affair with a gendarme, who had come to her hill village one winter following a murder in the wine cellar of the manor. The fetus did not want to be flushed out of her belly, neither with boiled keg wine, nor with burdock juice, nor with crushed gooseberries in pumpkin tea. And so, shortly before Easter, she fled to Buzau and from thence, by cart, on foot, however it happed, to Brăila, where she knew that a sister of her father lived, whom she had never seen in her life. She did not find her. Instead, she herself was found freezing, starving, dirty, and frightened, like a stray dog, by some Turks who were guarding a grain silo. She had made herself a nest at the peak of a mound of wheat, a few dozen feet in height, and was incessantly nibbling the hard, golden grains from the palm of her hand. And sometimes Allah is good, not like our Lord God, although He, too, can be good when it is a question of saving a wronged being, who, in just three or four days, after a few hot baths and human meals, is transformed into a pretty and hard-working lass, smiling and obedient. They chased her away some time later, when her belly had become large and irksome. A warm, mild autumn had come, so she was able to survive in the marshes, among the stagnant waters and rushes, learning how a wild cow can be milked if its calf is tethered to a willow or a poplar, how crayfish are drawn to the bank if they can smell carrion, how an old catfish can be caught in an eddy using a crucian carp as big as her palm, how to distinguish edible from poisonous mushrooms with the silver cross at her throat. She was in her seventh month and had no appetite for anything that did not lie beneath her eyes, but what she did see there she desired with all her heart: she trembled, shed tears, screamed, rolled in the clayey earth with its odor of mint and decay, prayed on her knees, tore out the hair that had grown down to her feet, and scratched her cheeks, and all for some duck's liver. A flock of wild ducks, as an unfathomable pause on their way to places without frost and icy north winds, had landed near her hut. Bluish-black, with comical tufts, sleek and raucous, there were so many that when they rose above the muddy pools they blackened the sky. Every time they took flight, not knowing whether they were leaving for good or merely moving a little farther on, in search of tepid water and shoals of fish, she would clench her fists in fury, until her fingernails made the skin of her palms burst and bleed. Far off, on the island, at the sandy end toward the town, there were a few houses and, from time to time, she would barter with the owners; she would give them caviar in return for twine and hooks, for matches she would tether unruly horses, she would go with a skirt full of blackberries, pounds of them, and return with a half a gallon of gas. From them, from those taciturn and scowling folk who looked at her as though she were a scarecrow, who mocked her and ceaselessly cheated her, she obtained two buckets of lees from a heap left by a plum-brandy still. In return she offered a three-foot-long pike, which was still moving. All afternoon, with the meticulousness of a girl who had been taught how to wind the raw silk from silkworm cocoons, to weave at the loom, and to plait loaves for funeral repasts, she had filled the bellies of fish with the fermented and long-distilled leftovers. Bleaks, redeyes, bream, and perch entered her wretched net, obtained a few weeks earlier in exchange for a live fawn. She groped for the ducks when it grew dark. They had gathered in throngs on a small lake sheltered from the wind, maybe as many as a thousand. They were already dozing. A weary quack could still be heard here and there. Stanca (whose name would never be known to the child she bore in her womb, although Tufty had dreamed of discovering it, Gherghe less so, and Onufrie not at all) approached noiselessly, became soaked and muddied up to the thighs creeping though the as-yet green reeds. She scattered over the water her alcoholic fish fry in a thin layer. The ducks did not sense her, and she experienced a long, sleepless night of expectation, during which she kept thinking and praying that her plan would work and during which the unborn child in her womb struggled as never before. In the morning, when the sun was about to rise, and the mist of the river was growing thinner, was unraveling in milky strips, the flock of ducks took flight for the last time, with a terrible flapping noise. She was not sorry, because she had collected forty-nine drunken birds. She tore them apart and ate their livers raw; she still had matches and splintered wood, but she no longer had patience. She washed the streaks of blood from her mouth and cheeks. Then she gave everything she had accumulated — the net, the gas, a blanket, and a smoke-blackened pan — to be ferried over the Danube. And she set out on foot over the fields of stubble toward her village on the hill. Somewhere on the way, in a willow wood, she gave birth to a boy. She wrapped him in a piece of white linen, which, since her time in Brăila, during her life at the silo, she had washed daily and laid out in the sun, on a bed of leaves and branches on the banks of a stream. She did not even notice that on his crown the infant had a tuft as long as his head.

After he had entered into full and exclusive ownership of an almost new beret (as it had been speciously described by the judge in Focshani whose eaves he had cleaned and for whom he had chopped two cartfuls of wood), Gherghe parted with his first hat, which was now as hard as tin. That payment for clambering onto the roof and swinging the ax had not been fortuitous, but rather he himself had insistently demanded it, to the wonderment of him who had paid it, a corpulent man, red in the cheeks, resembling in many respects Father Nae. Perhaps in the winter that followed, when the last of the firewood had burned up in the stove and when it could be expected that, in the shed, three thick tufts of bluish-black hair would have come to light, the magistrate might finally have understood something of the man's demand, but what did it matter? The hat from old biddy Vutza was not thrown in the rubbish, but on the evening of that same day, faded and battered as it

was, it had been laid to rest in the Mother Immaculate Cemetery beneath a well-tended tombstone with winsome cherubs at
the corners. On September 14, 1941, the sunset was purplish-
red in Focshani, a sign betokening wind, perhaps a storm, but
he did not see the colors of the sky or, if he did, he had no eyes
for them. He walked without stopping along the streets and
now and then rubbed his head, because he no longer felt the
wanted tightness on his brow and temples. He wore the checked
beret of soft felt for almost a year, until that town and all the
towns through which he passed, although places in which the
people knew nothing of his oddity or his old nickname, began
to seem cold and hypocritical to him, even hostile. He migrated
ceaselessly, always heading northeastward, unconsciously, for
in those parts, thanks to the course of history, space had opened
up and there was room enough to advance. He stopped at
Neamtz Monastery, not in homage to the calculations and alli-
ances of Marshal Antonescu, but to shelter from a cold rain
that had soaked him to the skin. And there he remained. At
first, wearing for a good few months the greenish-yellow
checked beret (which showed that the judge had once yearned
to become a golfer) the boy was a common servant, taking the
hermitage herd out to pasture, mucking out the stables, reaping
and stacking the hay, milking the cows, and transforming, by
means of a curved knife and a red-hot iron, bullocks into
worthy and obedient oxen. After his first confession to Father
Kalliop (who long remained his confessor, even after Marshal
Antonescu had been executed, the king had been forced to ab-
dicate, and the first secretary general had nationalized indus-
try), Gherghe was summoned by the abbot of the monastery,

Radifir, who insisted on touching his eight-inch tuft with his own fingers, on cutting it with the scissors he used to trim wicks, on checking its growth for one day, at four-hourly intervals, and on trying to burn it, in order to see whether it smelled of singed pig, which would have meant, and did mean, he was a poor lamb of the Lord, or whether it gave off a sulfurous miasma, which — God forbid! — would have indicated something else entirely. Immediately after that episode, the abbot gave him absolution to enter church with his head covered and ordered him no longer to cast away the tufts cut from his crown, but to gather them in a sack (six a day, forty-two a week, one hundred and eighty in April, June, September, and November, one hundred and eighty-six in the other seven months, and one hundred and sixty-eight in February, without taking into account leap years) and personally to surrender them to him, on the first calendar day of every month. What the abbot did with so much hair remained unclear to Gherghe. He renounced his worldly garb for the monastic habit in July 1943 and at the same time replaced his beret with a kamelavkion. This time, he did not go to the cemetery, but as a place of eternal rest for the checked cloth beret he chose a hollow in the bole of a beech, a solitary, shady tree that he knew from when he used to take the cattle to pasture. The kamelavkion was made from harsh frieze, so that Onufrie had to accustom himself to a constant and insufferable itch on his nape and above the ears. After the newest change of name, he also needed to accustom himself to other things. As a novice, he received a cup of red wine only on high feast days, and was forbidden mastika, raki, rye brandy, and plum brandy, which previously, during his wanderings and even in the monastery stables, he had drunk often and with pleasure; he was obliged to read for hours on end from the holy books, although at first he could barely tell the difference between the letters and it was impossible for him to trace them onto paper by himself; he discovered that hunger is torturous not only when you cannot find work and no one gives you alms, but also when you fast (caught one Friday evening in the henhouse, where he was eating raw eggs, he received thirty stinging switches on the bottom and was locked up for a week in a narrow cell); his legs would turn numb from kneeling, his middle would ache from the genuflections. He learned prayers and hymns full of incomprehensible words, his mouth would go dry uttering them, and his throat would ache. But sometimes he would vaguely sense something within them, perhaps in the rhythm, in a cadence or in a melody, perhaps in the mode of being and in the power of those to whom they were addressed—not even he could tell. It was something that warmed his chest like a hot tea, made his chin quiver, and even in the absence of candle smoke moistened his eyes. Brother Onufrie found himself then taking the first miraculous steps of love, but as the feeling had been alien to him for seventeen years, he made up for time lost and bore himself like a child ready to aggravate and pester the creature dear to it. Once, in church, taking a break from scrubbing the floor, he slowly pierced with his scissors the left thigh of the Child, as He was slumbering at the breast of the Mother. It was on the eve of the Feast of Michael and Gabriel, and the next day, under the tutelage of the two archangels, he commenced a long and arduous road to gain forgiveness, at the end of which he saw more the Virgin Mary and less Jesus. Meanwhile, he was to place hundreds of bouquets of flowers by that icon, to say thousands of prayers before it, and tenaciously to wet with his tears the mat on which he knelt, until it acquired a stain of putrefaction at one of its corners. However, it was something else that affected the rhythm of his life after he became a monk. Present at matins, at vespers, at midnight and other services, following a strict timetable of reading and meals, he had been obliged to modify the hours at which he cut his tuft. Before he settled into the new rhythm, sometimes seven or eight hours would pass between two trimmings of the bunch on his crown, and so he had discovered what happened to his hair if it was left to its own devices. It rapidly turned white, became pulpy, then oozed like molten wax, scorching the skin of his scalp and causing a pain like the toothache. What is curious is that, precisely during that period of bodily sufferings, when he had to solve a by no means simple mathematical problem, how to divide twenty-four hours into six equal periods, Onufrie found the meaning of joy. It was not a chronic state, nor could it have been: there were rare moments, impossible to anticipate or conserve, in which he was not thinking of anything in particular, had nothing to do with persons or deeds, moments in which everything, in a physical sense, emptied out of him, and that emptiness was filled with something else indefinable. He would then forget about the itch on his nape and above his ears, about sleep, about the severe gaze of Abbot Radifir, about some of the monks' game with she-rabbits thrust into the narrow cage of the he-rabbit, about the lisping speech of Father Kalliop, about the taste of the pickled-cabbage soup, about the yellowing, stained pages of the breviaries, about the smell of wild strawberry jam and fresh whey, about monastic labors and intrigues and about countless other things. And how good that was.

Between the time of kamelavkion of rough frieze and the time of straw hat (bought from a market a few years after the final secretary general was shot), he also wore a soldier's cap, without a five-pointed star or other symbol; a worn-out shawl; a black kidskin hat; a canvas cap; and once again a kamelavkion, wholly different from the first, made of soft cloth, pleasant to the touch, and lined with satin. Each of these marked a stage in his life. The soldier's cap, faded and lacking in military insignia as it was, indicates the period of hard labor immediately following the removal of young men from the monasteries in order to be cured of mysticism. The shawl, with its feminine resonance, with the inclination toward travesty, is the symbol of his escape from the mine and flight through territories dotted with patrols and checkpoints. The fur hat has a deceptive tinge, it carries the thoughts away to hunting, that is, to bloodshed, but, ever since he had pierced the left thigh of the Holy Child with his scissors he had fervently been seeking forgiveness and would have done no harm to any creature. (Later, as a hieromonk, when a good Christian woman had said to him in astonishment and slight disgust that he had a louse in his white beard, Onufrie had replied, "Eh, it, too, is a creature of the Lord.") In fact, that strange head covering, fashioned inside-out from the fur of a kid found dead among the rocks, recalls his long period as a hermit, seeking hiding places in the mountains. The canvas cap did not protect the tuft of bluish-black hair for long, but it is a sign of Gherghe's reconciliation with the world, at the moment when he was able to emerge from mountain caves and forests, having learned that his conviction had been erased along with the others, and that this was called an amnesty. Then followed the second kamelavkion, so handsome and comfortable, which not only made his monastic standing official once more but also permitted him to live in the place from whence, two decades previously, he had been uprooted at gunpoint and thrown, alongside the other brothers, into a truck with a khaki tarpaulin. As for his wide-brimmed straw hat, with which he is now seen in the glade at Red Rock, where he has already built and painted the murals of a small chapel next to a fir tree with nine crowns and where, aided by disciples with budding beards and with buckets, he is now striving to erect a church and a few monastic cells, it is the proof, or at least the consequence, of *the third descent of the Mother of God from the heavens to show Her succor and faith in Onufrie.*

⟶⟵

And what explains the multitude of scars? The index finger of his right hand, the one he so often raised and shook with such zeal, was not full of ordinary cuts, gained unwittingly during labor or who knows how else, but rather, from base to tip, on its fleshy side, it was furrowed by dozens of small, horizontal lines. All were the work of his own hand, the left, of course, and had been made with his indispensible scissors, the well-sharpened scissors with which, six times a day, he cut the tuft on his crown, and with which, long ago, on the eve of the feast of the Archangels Michael and Gabriel, he had disturbed the sleep of the infant Christ at the breast of the Virgin. Each incision, closing in time and transformed into a thin stripe, measured one more year elapsed since *the second descent of the Mother of God from the heavens to show Her succor and faith in Onufrie*. Whereas others celebrated their birthdays in the houses of their birth (which in his case was impossible), he had begun to notch his finger, in the mountains on May 16, exactly a year after the Virgin Mary had made Her appearance next to a group of prisoners just emerging from a mine and, without being seen or heard by anyone else, either by the guards or his comrades, She had urged him fearlessly to traverse the empty courtyard, and to hide in a wagon. Now the lines on his finger, packed closely together, even overlapping, were uncountable, but there must have been around fifty.

SMALL MARSUPIAL, RELATED to the koala, six letters, with a *b* in the middle. It must be a *b*, because the word across is the capital of Australia, which is Canberra. Apart from that, nothing . . . What was that there? Maybe I'll get the first letter from that other word across. Bird . . . national symbol of New Zealand. Hmm, I don't know! And it's twenty to three in the morning! God! He takes off his glasses and leaves them on the nightstand. He rubs his forehead with his palms; he runs his fingers through his thinning white hair, combed over his pate. He opens a box of diazepam and swallows a third tablet. Before getting out of bed, Titus Maeriu, retired engineer, author of a doctoral thesis on tunnel resistance in strata of sedimentary rock, leading member of an association of former political prisoners, descendant of a long line of Uniate priests, father of two girls, grandfather of five grandchildren, and great-grandfather of an angelic little boy, bent once more over the magazine and with two thick lines underscored the title of that recalcitrant crossword: "Down Under." In the bathroom mirror he observes a large, reddish blotch on one cheek. He examines it carefully. It is not an irritation, or eczema. He soon realizes that it is a mark left by the pillow: he had lain propped in the same position for too long. He rinses his dentures and drops them into the glass of chamomile infusion on the edge of the sink. He urinates calmly—thank God the prostate operation turned out reasonably well! And after flushing the water he observes yet again how restful a hotel room can be when the cistern of the water closet does not purl incessantly. Turning toward the bed, Mr. Maeriu thinks that, if he is going to stay here for some time, and it seems that he will (it is impossible for him to believe that in just a few days they will establish what is what with those bones), he will be obliged, after having fixed that wretched toilet-cistern float, to repair the door lock too: not only was it very hard to insert the key into the keyhole, but also, in order to turn it in one direction or the other, much exertion was required. In any case, it is impossible for him to sleep. He is too hot with the blanket, but with just the sheet he is too cold. With the window closed it is suffocating, there is no air, but with it open he cannot stand the draft, and the distant but frequent noise of the trains throngs his mind with too many things, not one of which is appealing. As for laughter, his youngest daughter still laughs neither more rarely, nor more often, the same as ever, but something has changed on that scale between smile and chortle, not in intensity, not in sonority, but somewhere else. Laughter is either full or hollow, just as a hazelnut either does or does not have a kernel. Hers is a regular laugh, without shamming, but for a good few years the fruit has been withering, inside the husk. He sees a little girl of eight or nine, running, with long thin pigtails dancing above her shoulders, she has unusually large eyes, they are burning, her laughter flows in incessant waves, they stream one after another and overtake her and caress the lambs she cannot manage to catch. It must have been March or April, but to Titus, at five to four in the morning, it looks like the middle of July, because the outlines of the little girl and the lambs are superimposed upon a sea of harvest-time flowers. For an instant he senses the scent of fresh hay, he is sweating, he casts the blanket aside, he immediately feels cold and is once again wrapping himself up when the girl's pigtails vanish and are replaced by a willfully youthful coiffure, but one which, in spite of the good intentions of curling tongs and hair dye, does not manage to conceal age. The eyes too have changed, they remain hazel, but they no longer burn, often they are icy. The little girl no longer chases after lambs, not because she is not in good physical shape—she is, she does aerobics a number of times a week—but the little girl has known too much: love, mathematics, Easter lamb pudding, high and flat heels, the throes of labor, driving, divorce. Mr. Maeriu sees a pale line of light at the peak of the little mountain across the valley, for the time being it is blue, timid. He regards it without emotion, this time he knows, rather than suspects, that laughter may exist even where sadness has forever made its nest. The hotel room is insipid, apart from its number, 419, there is nothing that could make you remember it, but it nonetheless has an advantage: it is not infested by rats, nor is it invaded by swarms of mosquitoes. Mildew is also lacking from the walls. This room could not provide better proof that, compared to calamity, mediocrity is worth its weight in gold. It is a tonic observation, because, since he has been taking part in the investigations regarding the mass grave, Titus has sometimes, though rarely, wondered whether the unfortunates who found eternal rest there have not somehow been more favored than he. He had arrived in the small mountain town as an official representative of former political prisoners, as a sign that the survivors of the prisons venerate those who died and, above all, in order to show the association's lack of trust in an inquiry conducted by prosecutors who were schooled by the old torturers. He did not doubt that many of those ribs and vertebrae—those tibias, femurs, and fibulas, the four, seven, fifteen clavicles, the who knows how many kneecaps, an ulna here, a radius and a humerus there, a sternum at the surface of the heap, a sacrum toward the bottom, bones large and small, hosts of them, yellowish-white, waxen, moldering, impersonal—and the skulls, above all the skulls, once belonged, mid-century, to young men recalcitrant like so many others, men who were not to discover the sickly taste of domesticity, of world-weariness, even of betrayal. What fate had the greater worth, on whose part had the luck been? Beyond the valley, the river and the railway line, the sky is growing rosy, the dawn puts an end to yet another sleepless night and somewhere presses on the heart, heavily, just as the blade of a pickax once pressed against the veins of his left wrist, long ago, at Cape Midia, beneath a washed-out February sunrise while the guards were gathered around a fire and he wanted to end his life. Mr. Maeriu lightly strokes the scar, he passes his fingertips over the kinks of the skin, he rises from bed, readies the pot and the elements to boil the water for a caffeine-free coffee, and cannot understand why Petrus, the archaeologist, otherwise such an educated and big-hearted boy, is taking the side of such suspect individuals as the three prosecutors and the coroner. Also, he cannot for the life of him understand why wee Răzvan, such a sweet little boy, a little prince, will not, at the age of almost three, do his number ones and his number twos in his potty.

⤚⤜

Oh, what cheap deodorant—sweet, too sweet, overpowering! And what insufferable stubble, you'd think it was emery paper! Caterina keeps her eyes shut, her head lolls to one side, with difficulty she stops him touching her face and chest, she can already see her skin overrun with a throng of bluish-red spots, she imagines that her lips will end up in tatters if they fall prey to that greedy mouth. She feels strong palms running over her thighs, her body remains hostile, she thinks that it is not enough to carry condoms in her purse: she also ought to carry a good men's eau de cologne and, above all, a razor, with plenty of spare blades. She puts a stop to the caresses with a firm movement. She twists around and takes two small sips from the glass of wine on the nightstand. She leans against the headboard of the bed and lights a cigarette. Through the open window, she can see a scrap of moon; she does not even observe how swiftly the clouds obscure it. She scrutinizes the label on the pinot noir and wonders whether 1992 was a dry or a rainy year. His fingers have reached somewhere below her knees. They have given up their frenzy, and they appear to be resting. They gently stretch and clench, now and then they run up and down the leg, but each time they return and resume their torpor. The bottle inclines and dark wine fills Caterina's glass, the glass approaches Caterina's lips, and the dark wine tickles her tongue, Caterina's tongue contracts like a snail into its shell and the dark wine vanishes, allowing the image of vel-

vet to form, vaguely at first, then ever more clearly. A hand
pauses in close-cropped hair, the bathrobe, clothing a naked
body, is laid aside, the cold night air, coming through the open
window, is reminiscent not of snow or the water of a mountain
lake, but of an endless, yellowish expanse of velvet. It glides
over the pillow, the other hand descends to one of her breasts,
from the ashtray comes the smell of burnt filter-tip, the chest
and arms that clasp her exude that sickly sweet odor and another, new one—bitter, pungent. Her sense of smell has lost
its vigilance, it has loaned all its virtues to the sense of touch,
Caterina shrills like a mouse. Her lips have opened, have blos-
somed, they softly ascend a shoulder, then a neck, a prickly
cheek, they find the earlobe and do not release it until high-
pitched sounds (they might be called sighs, but they are not
quite sighs) overlie the jerky rumbling of a train in the valley. She is gradually overwhelmed by the cold, a cold that is
ever more piercing, while Luci's silver earring, still wet, loses
its shine, becomes matte as it dries. She rises and sits at the
edge of the bed, the bathrobe lies crumpled in a ball between
the sheets, the pinot noir now seems too harsh, undrinkable.
She looks at the clock, it's twenty to three in the morning! Go!
And, without too much politeness, she asks to be left alone.
She would have liked a jet of hot water to lash her back, but
the hotel shower can only offer her something lukewarm, lacking in vigor, a kind of tepid drizzle from which she has to flee
as quickly as possible. She is already in front of the mirror,
the droplets gleam on her purplish-white skin, she is shivering,
the towel cannot hide what she knows in detail and chronically
hates: a dumpy body, without ankles or waist, with lengths and
widths the wrong way round, a weary, pallid face with wilt-

ing make-up. It is slightly better under the blanket; the hotel bed is no great shakes, but it is still a bed. By the light of the lamp, she leafs through the previous day's paper, the newspaper for which she works. She is certain that the latest issue has been off the press for quite some time; it must already be on its way to the kiosks and stands. For the third time she reads her own article and at last she has warmed up, that short and plump body no longer preoccupies her, the dark wine no longer rivals velvet, nor does it now seem off. How great that characterization is! "The three prosecutors sent with orders to bury the mass grave." And how clearly she put it! "The former political prisoners will not accept the transformation of a crime into a circus." Somewhere in the middle of room 306, on a table — and Caterina casts a fleeting glance at it — there stands a bouquet of forget-me-nots that Titus Maeriu gave her yesterday, that little old man who has come to take part in the whole affair, a man who, for all his clacking dentures, understands that a woman cannot be reduced to svelte legs and an appetizing figure. Her eyelids are heavy, but she is not ready to close them yet. She takes one more sip from the glass and turns to her latest, handwritten dispatch, the one that will be printed in this morning's paper. It is about the coroner, about his haste to confirm all the presuppositions of the three prosecutors. Her short text — twenty-one lines, that's how much the editor asked for — pursues the idea that only an individual liable to blackmail, with grave blots in his past record but otherwise an expert, could claim that he has not identified in so many bodily remains (bones upon bones, mounds, heaps!) a single trace of violent death. If she sat with her eyes toward the window, Caterina would see a milky streak emerging above the woods, she would see how the stars are fading, but she is sitting looking at the ceiling and clearly discerns, from somewhere behind it, the outline of the coroner, with an unusually large bottom for a man, with hips broader than his shoulders, an outline that is beige, like his customary suit. She throws the small manuscript onto the floor—that's how much the editor asked for, twenty-one lines—she extinguishes the lamp, and curls up under the blanket. By chance her right hand touches her left breast. There it comes to rest. One thought is still awake: in three days it will be her thirty-third birthday and, not by chance, on that very day the head of the paper's socioeconomic section will also arrive in town on delegation. It will be the first time that she and Patzi, without caring about colleagues, readers, his wife, his kids, and his grandchildren, will have sex in a bed. Not on desks, not among the typewriters, not with the door locked.

⤛⤜

The wind is chilly, and it has a taste, a taste of mulberries. The boat passes by a white poplar. Over the water hang scattered streaks of haze, whelps of mist. The boat leaves behind a row of dwarf willows. A bluish-black night, like ink! He advances against a darkened backdrop of colorless grasses and bushes. Ah, how agile is his little wooden boat! Not even the current opposes it. The night is tranquil, but much can be heard on the banks, sounds that not every ear can detect: a faint whistle, rustling, a flutter, more fluttering, cracking brushwood. Andryusha deciphers them one by one. A lapwing, a muskrat, a pair of bald coots, a pig. The river air fills his chest; it percolates fresh and sweet into his belly, into his arms and thighs. It is as though he is breathing with his entire body, he becomes lighter, very light, he too takes flight above the Katsavaya channel of the Danube delta, along with the gossamers. Later, he is in the boat once again, he is crossing an expanse of reeds, he is standing and thrusting with his pole into the muddy water's bottom, the morning star is right before his eyes, and he cries, *"Kak sebye, krasavitsa!? Lyubimaya!"* And, as he drinks, all in one gulp, from a bottle of vodka, a bottle that has come into his hands he knows not how, he feels the wondrous star draw the longboat through the marshes, giving it the power to advance whither it wishes. He has reached the mouth of a small lake, not at all deep: it is a pond just right for catching crabs in springtime. Before him lies a pound net, one alone, one of his new pound nets. He recognizes it immediately by the knife notch made on the hornwood rings and by the knots on the line. He hastens to raise it and empty it in the boat, but as soon as he touches it, he feels it shaking. The net resists; heavy, taut, it is about to slip through his fingers. He is panting, his head is wet, soaking wet; it is as though raindrops stream through the pores of his skin and through the roots of his hair. He looks for the bottle to take a few more slugs of vodka, but it has vanished without a trace. He looks up at the morning star, but he no longer finds it in the heavens, in its place has appeared the worried face of his grandma Lyuba. *"Babushka! Babushka!"* The wind now tastes of mulberry tarts. Andryusha is sure that he has caught a large fish. He spits and starts to sing softly, with a trembling voice, *"Oy, Moroz, Moroz."* Grasped with care, the net obeys him little by little, it tightens, rises, the wooden rings draw closer, the creature beneath the water is struggling with all its might, it could be a huge, rebellious pike, or an old sheatfish, longer than his older sister, Verochka.

The pound net suddenly vanishes and in his hand he is holding the purse net. He has succeeded, the fish is caught, but what he finds there is not a fish, maybe it is an otter, an otter that entered the net after a small fry, but nor is it an otter, it is something whitish, inert, it is not a living creature because it is not struggling, it is a thing or a collection of things, the weight is breaking his arms. He now sees clearly that what has been caught in his net is a host of human bones, only the skulls, five or six. Andryusha sings no more, he has been struck dumb, his silence is short, then he screams, screams shrilly, and the one who wakes up in the hotel corridor, on the second floor, Private Andrey Butylkin, on guard in front of room 211, is bathed in sweat, it is as though someone had drenched him with a garden hose. He looks around him bewildered. The corridor is empty. A neon light drones uninterruptedly. On the window of the fire hose cabinet someone has stuck a piece of chewing gum. A few moths are trying to enter by the window on his right, the one with the view toward the mountains. He wipes his brow with the sleeve of his tunic, lifts himself up from the grimy carpet. He is numb; his back is hurting, somewhere below the ribs. He lights a cigarette. From behind the door, from within the room of the person he is supposed to be guarding, footfalls can be heard. The key turns in the lock, the handle is pressed down, and the figure of military prosecutor Spiru appears: two bleary eyes, sharp cheekbones, and a broad mouth above a pair of brown pajamas, with the lapel button torn off. Private Butylkin hears, "What? What? What's happened?" He answers that he was dreaming, hears a curse, makes no response, and sees the door slamming in his face. He looks at his watch. It is twenty to three in the morning! God! Where did the time go?

It won't be long before the last man on duty turns up. He paces up and down the long, dimly lit corridor, once, twice, eight, fourteen, twenty-six turns, then who knows how many, he has lost count, the walking does him good, the twinge in his back has gone, and the image of the net no longer frightens him. He has seen plenty of human bones lately and he will see them again the next day and the day after that and so on, when they will be taken to that blasted mass grave yet again, an entire platoon of gendarmes. In the end, that's fine: that's not labor, working with a trowel instead of a shovel, with little plastic bags instead of sacks and wheelbarrows, with all kinds of rest breaks, when the prosecutors start quarreling or when the coroner gets another bright idea or when the chief of police shows up, that puffball as red as a boiled crab. Oho, and how good the walls, the ruins, are! You can slip into town straightaway, to get some booze, cigarettes, or a loaf of bread. You can sneak off to the edge of the woods and have a quick nap, or at least stretch out in the grass, in the shade, after the lieutenant puts on his spectacles and starts reading the papers. Rather than drill and alerts at the barracks, rather than weeks on guard duty, six hours at your post, six awake, six asleep or, even worse, six on, six off and nothing in between, without any sleep, when who knows what's going on, it is better to put up with Spiru. He's maimed, he's a spook, he's a bastard, he shouts, he waves his arms about like someone possessed, his eyes bulge out, at ten o'clock at night you have to stand guard at his door, he's convinced their commandant that he's in danger and needs a guard. You never escape without polishing the magistrate colonel's shoes or without brushing his uniform. You curse him in your mind, and after that you get over it. It's worth getting over it at least for that little old man who keeps walking among them and jotting things down in a blue notebook, but not anything bad, as they had believed at first, because the lieutenant didn't punish anyone for talking to him, that little old man who every single day manages to rile the prosecutors, especially Spiru, that little old man, the political prisoner, the one who gives cigarettes to anyone who asks and who once, on the Day of the Dead, at the twelve o'clock call, with the lieutenant present, laid an entire crate of wine in front of the platoon. Butylkin leans his elbows on the windowsill. Somewhere high up, far away, a light gleams. He has heard that there is a cabin up there. He has sworn that he will never go there. He can't stand these mountains, any mountains. What was the meaning of the star in his dream? It was the morning star, which transformed into his grandma Lyuba. *"Babushka! Babushka!"* He could eat five trays of mulberry tarts on the spot.

→>◅←

There is no need for a freeze-frame, because in room 211, with the exception of a tiny spider, nothing is moving. The window is closed, the curtains are drawn, the currents of air are faint, they could not even budge the scrunched-up paper napkin on the table, a white napkin with little lilac pine trees, soiled by the chocolate glaze of an éclair. The image is constant, unconnected to time: a body in a pose of deep slumber, the left arm following the diagonal of the bed, the right hanging to the floor, the legs bent and slightly apart, in an equestrian attitude, one cheek buried in the pillow, and the other left to the mercy of the night, for shadows of every shape and form to settle on the jutting cheekbone, making it seem, against the crinkled expanse of skin, now a molehill, now a rock rearing from the sea, now a heap of coal. This picture might be titled *The Dreamless Sleep of the Magistrate Colonel* or *The Sleeping Man of Law*. His substance is profoundly static. The conventional term *still life* is also apposite, since in this nocturnal state military prosecutor Spiru exhibits the properties of an inert object rather than those of a living being. The chromatics are gray, except that everything is situated on the edge of pitch darkness, the only sources of light being the yellowish streak beneath the door and the Russian alarm clock, equipped with a minuscule bulb. And there are yet more details. Two of the digits of the left hand, the middle and ring fingers, are touching the bedside table, splayed over its shiny surface, another two, the index finger and thumb, dangle into space, like ripe fruits, while the fifth finger, the little finger, is quite simply missing, with only the stump at the base of the phalanx to prove that it ever existed. The finger is nevertheless present within the frame, in the form of a yellowed little bone, just like the bones large and small that fill the mass grave within the perimeter of the Roman fort. This little bone is privileged, however, as it has become a permanent amulet or lucky charm for its owner, hanging from his neck by a silver chain. Somewhere in the cupboard (the picture also allows us to see a number of things that are, as a rule, invisible), hidden in a pouch behind the colonel's eleven white shirts, can be found many, very many other little fingers, collected with limitless abnegation from that mass grave. To each is tied a scrap of paper, on which are inscribed their length and girth, measured with precision (beneath the bundle of eleven white shirts gleams a pair of calipers), and on which can be read the spontaneous thoughts of the military magistrate, noted

on the occasion of each new item being added to the collection.
These are short, barely legible texts, a few of which can be deciphered: "Prison? Hard labor? They should all be executed!
All of them! Bastards!" "My head is aching! My head is aching really badly!" ". . . and so here comes this jailbird and starts
telling me what to do . . ." "So what if I did put a bullet in your
forehead, you rat?! You made like you were out cold after the
beating, didn't you? You bit me and stole my finger . . . So now
I'm stealing their fingers, you rat!" "Life's a piece of shit! My
head is aching!" Another detail relates to the spider. (The picture does not restrict movement, nor deform its rhythm and its
spaces.) It is a reckless insect, smaller than a pea, that has ventured to traverse the ceiling, from the pelmet positioned above
the window toward the photograph showing the Iron Gates
Dam, with the same bravado with which the Spanish naviga-
tors of old once roved the open seas. It has sixteen legs, but
seems particularly to find purchase and strength in the frontal
and dorsal pairs. Its stripy garb, with light brown streaks on a
dark brown ground, is also somewhat similar, albeit not at the
chromatic level, to the uniform of the mariners envisaged. The
spider has no mind to spin a web, neither hunger nor hunting,
not even instinct let alone practicality seems to preoccupy it.
Everything is a matter of effort, of orientation, of tenacity. Its
voyage is accompanied somewhere below, in the region of the
bed (the picture does not suppress sounds, nor does it muffle
them), by a peculiar snoring. The squashed nose of the prosecutor, with its large, flared nostrils, has very little to do with
these noises, it is rather the mouth that releases them to flood
the room. What can be heard, if the points of reference were
to be zoological, however richly inclusive (animals exotic or

native, wild or domestic, terrestrial or aquatic, flying or flight-less), does not resemble, as is generally the case, the language of pigs, it does not, in fact, resemble anything known to man. When the spider at last reaches the western extremity of the ceiling and vanishes wearily behind the photograph of the Iron Gates Dam, the snoring ceases and a scream comes from the other side of the door. The colonel leaps from bed, turns on the light (the picture dissolves), and, wearing his pajamas with the button near the collar torn off, hurriedly exits into the hotel corridor. There he discovers a scrawny soldier puffing bleary-eyed on a cigarette, a frightened young man who explains to him that he had a bad dream. He swears at him and vanishes. The alarm clock—Oho! How much time has passed since he bought it! In Leningrad, when he was a student—indicates twenty to three in the morning. What a piece of shit!

CHAPTER FIVE

✦➤◄✦

For auntie paulina, the enigma foretold by the coffee grounds was elucidated in an unexpected manner. On the wall under the kitchen sink, a moldy stain had been spreading, droplets were seeping through cracks, and so she had to call a plumber. A garrulous old duffer aged about sixty arrived, who kissed her hand and did not decline a glass of cherry liqueur, an amiable little fellow who called her "ma'am" (and she was not annoyed) and who, before getting down to work, laid out so many tools and accessories that you would have thought it was a surgical intervention. Firstly, though not before putting on his gloves, he used a little hammer and a fine carpenter's chisel for softwood. After he had stripped the wall of the ripe layer of loam, he proceeded to use a piece of sandpaper, then pliers, with which he removed the last remnants of paint. When he reached the lime plasterwork, reeking of damp, he rose from his crouching position, sighed, and shook his head: "Ma'am, it's bad! The leak has done its job, it's probably a lead pipe . . ." Paulina sighed too, "Likely, dear, likely . . ." And she sat down helpless on a chair, with her hands in her lap. The little fellow praised the cherry liqueur (in order to oblige Auntie to pour him another), took a sip, licked his lips, and selected a putty knife from among his countless instruments. He explained to us

that shocks and blows should be avoided, and predicted that at
a given moment, if pensions didn't go up, that lot would have
to start importing old folk soon, not just natural gas and grain.
He was slowly scraping away the plaster, talking about his latest telephone bill and the cost of doctors, when a clink was
heard. From the wall, between his hands, a grimy coin fell to
the floor and rolled as far as the kitchen door. It was a golden
cockerel. It had undoubtedly been minted under Napoleon III.
It had the required Gallic engraving and, at least originally, had
circulated with a value of twenty francs. However, Auntie Paulina had no need of such numismatic niceties, but rather of water and valerian, while the old duffer, likewise uninterested in
historical details, swiftly drained two glasses of cherry liqueur
and picked up his hammer. The pipe was indeed made of lead
and was fissured, but what did it matter? In a frying pan (the
first capacious object that came to hand) Paulina collected 186
coins. She was squealing like a schoolgirl ("Look, dearie, look!
Just let me see you laugh now! You didn't believe me! The
fortunetelling . . . and the dreams . . . Just let me catch you saying they're all nonsense!"), she was crawling on all fours, she
went under the table and stretched out on her tummy to look
under the cupboard with the crockery and under the refriger-
ator, she herself started scooping out the damp, friable mortar with a spoon, she tapped the brickwork to make sure there
were no more hollow spots, and then, all of a sudden, she put
the frying pan, money and all, on top of the range and sank
into a chair. She was trembling. And she was pale. The plumber
had put down his glass, he was leaning with his back against the
windowsill, his arms dangling, and looking wide-eyed at the

gray hole under the sink. He asked me for a cigarette and, halfway through (Auntie was no longer in the kitchen—she had gone to my room, where she kept her nuptial photograph, the one with the "I. F. Kissling, Ploesci, Photo-Globe" crest, and where she could speak to Jorgu and thank him at will), he confessed to me that he had given up smoking nineteen years ago. He was puffing away like a schoolboy making his first foray with tobacco, and continually tapping the ash. A little later, he received from Paulina an unopened bottle of cherry liqueur and five gleaming coins, which she had chosen at random and rubbed on the sleeve of her dressing gown. That evening, when we were alone, Auntie cleaned the cockerels with toothpaste and a toothbrush. She examined them on both sides, bit a few of them, produced from who knows where a damask tablecloth and, on the white fabric, arranged them in a circle, in a triangle, and in all kinds of other geometric shapes. She traced jagged lines and spirals with them, tried to stack them in twos, threes, fours, and so on, until she grew tired and realized that she would never manage to divide them perfectly. I then explained to her (I too was on my third glass of cherry liqueur) how divisibility works and what a prime number means. She looked at me as though I was in fairyland, especially since I had stubbornly refused ("You're a mule, that's what you are!" she said) to be in any way rewarded. For the first time since I had been lodging there, she knocked on my door after I had got into bed. I was not asleep. She opened the door a crack, not even enough to fit her head, and whispered, "What is it with you and that archaeology, dear, in those old forts you can't even find what you find here in the kitchen . . ."

Thanks to the treasure that came out of the wall many things happened in a short time, even if Auntie only partially followed the plans made that chilly Wednesday when the coffee grounds had announced that she would receive an unexpected sum of money. Auntie Paulina behaved in a moderate and God-fearing way. She took the cockerels to the bank and changed them into today's Romanian lei. She opened a checking account and set up a number of deposit accounts with varying rates of interest (as the clerk, a young man fascinated by his own necktie, had advised). She looked after her family according to the simple logic of blood being thicker than water and of the bond before the altar. She wired significant sums to her sister Lucica and her nephew Virgil, the one whom she had dreamed was being lured by a redheaded woman. As was to be expected, the two telephoned on the very same day the postwoman rang their doorbell and drove away their plentiful financial problems. They tried to be as nice as possible, but after Auntie's replies they must have been left with furrowed brows, since she avoided any discussion as to the provenance of the money. Toward the end of the conversation, she asked Lucica to put off the visit she had been planning, explaining that she herself was going on a journey. She could not renounce what she had clearly read in the cup: she was now treating the signs in the coffee grounds as commandments. However, before setting off, before even choosing a destination or deciding upon other details of the voyage (duration, means of transport, how many stars the hotels and boarding houses would have, and a few other things), Paulina tended to Jorgu's grave. She replaced the old cross, cast in concrete from an insipid mold much used throughout the cemetery, with one hewn from white marble, which bore not only his name and his ceramic photograph but also hers: a sleek cross, upon which the stonemason had chiseled a line from Ştefan O. Iosif: "And the mists rise from black valleys." It was a line from the deceased's favorite poem and as much as could be enigmatically and eternally preserved from pastoral tableaux with mournful cowbells, "a kind of censorship of death, dear," as Auntie had explained to me. She had surrounded the eternal resting place with a squat fence of wrought iron and covered the grave with zinnias and dwarf dahlias.

She went out of the door early one Thursday morning, ready to board the bus that stopped at the entrance to the park and whose final destination was Greece (she said Mount Olympus, in order to abide by that letter O three times present in the coffee grounds). It was cloudy and windy. I once more expressed concern as to the weight of her luggage and insisted on taking her to the bus stop. She did not object, as she had the evening before. We both knew that my assistance had nothing to do with the suitcase, which reeked of naphthalene, but with her nerves. At the bus stop, there was someone else waiting for the coach to Athens: the lady doctor from the sanatorium, head of the TB section, a woman of almost fifty, short and thin, whom Paulina greeted cordially, although they knew each other only to the extent that everybody recognizes everybody else in a small provincial town. When the other woman moved a little to one side, to check the locks on her suitcase, Auntie whispered to me that once again the predictions in the coffee cup were being fulfilled, inasmuch as she would not have a solitary journey. How happy she was, in fact, that she would not be alone! She begged me once again to seek out and listen to Dumitru M., Paraschiva's husband, and bathed in perspiration she set off to the soothing air of the Mediterranean.

❧❧❧

It is a blessing to be alone with Jojo in a small and tidy house, in many respects the house of an old woman, but with freshly whitewashed walls, three windows facing west toward a beech tree puffed up like a turkey, another two looking south, with roses and a blossoming jasmine bush in front, with a shady veranda where rocking chairs idled, and a small skylight, through which seeped the sunset. It has to be in summertime, near the solstice (and it was), for it is only then that the sun clears the mountain and streams through that triangular pane in the roof. There are yellowish or reddish streaks on the ceiling: in order to appreciate their motion and intensity you need to lie sprawling on your back, on the floor or in one of the rocking chairs, to hold Josephina tightly in your arms, and not to depart from that place or from that embrace until twilight comes. The colors spattered against the white background are reminiscent of cherries, blackberries, or pomegranates, but when your skin adheres to hers, when a bead of sweat trickles down her back, right down her spine, and in it the twilight sparkles, when on one of her knees there appears a blotch from where your elbow has pressed, when on her throat the Adam's apple quivers, and her belly button tightens, then there appear one after the other plums, melons, strawberries and green grapes, apricots and apples, and mulberries, and many, many more. Paulina's rocking chairs have a slight creak, but it can no longer be heard when the sun is extinguished like a light bulb, all of a sudden, and when Jojo spreads her fingers like a fan. And each day ends with its sunset, with Jojo and me shut up in Auntie's house, while the latter is visiting temples, monasteries, and bays of water so pellucid that her ailing, age-wearied, and myopic eyes can distinguish the dance of the seaweed above the shellfish, above crabs, above fish that arouse in her culinary appetites, a dance ennobled by the sparkling particles of sand that have absorbed, at another place and another hour, something of another sun. Eugenia Embury, whom I often saw in the neighboring yard, especially in the morning, when she used to water the flowers (and snap off the withered petals, and examine the buds, and root out the vigorous and impudent shoots of weeds), thought that her granddaughter was away in Bucharest to sit an important exam. Even from a distance peace could be read upon her face, and when she took a cat in her arms or when she summoned them all to table, for us, in the absence of the brandy, a new occasion would arise to take a sip of tea in homage. My ulcer was doing better. It may have been that a young woman's clothes strewn around the house had a therapeutic effect unknown to doctors. However, my reserves of cigarettes were almost depleted, and so I searched in the bag of socks in the wardrobe. I found there a packet of Viceroys (I was like a squirrel who forgets where he has hidden his store), but also an envelope on which Auntie Paulina had inscribed my name in large rounded letters. Inside it there were twenty-two gold coins, minted under Napoleon III, whose initial value in circulation had been twenty-two francs. Perhaps Auntie Paulina had understood how divisibility works, perhaps she had been thinking of Jojo's age. Whatever it might have been, now we had cigarettes!

⤛⤜

Just as the pharmacist's passion for *The Lives of the Saints* was no secret to anybody (every day she would inscribe on patients' prescriptions the name of the saint celebrated on that date in the Orthodox calendar, adding summary descriptions, full of abbreviations, of the sufferings endured or the miracles worked by the sanctified), just as Mr. Sasha's aversion to cows (ever since his dromedary had been castrated) and the postman's surrender to the sin of drink (after his wife had mistaken turpentine for holy water and left him with four children to raise, two in elementary school and two in kindergarten) were known to all, just as everyone knew that the Pilot, who had been party secretary at an airbase and was now a colonel in the reserve, had never flown, so too Dumitru M. had his own public dossier, abundant in data. He was the oldest person in the town—some said ninety-four, others ninety-seven, plenty of voices swore that he was over a hundred, and it was even supposed that he was about to reach a hundred and eight. He wore a hat and a necktie whenever he went outside. He used a walking stick. He still went to the cinema, although he regularly fell asleep, regardless of the subject of the film and however noisy the soundtrack might be. He had not gone bald. He ate much and heartily, as testified by the women behind the counter of the neighborhood grocery store, where he bought bacon, eggs, pork livers and kidneys, marmalade and walnuts, and on rare occasions fish, but only when herring was in season. As a subject of the king, he had owned a tile and fire-clay factory and a few oil fields (two or three retired policemen swore that in his driving license, issued in '34 or '35, his profession was given as "industrialist"), while under the Communists, as foreman of the faience-making team at the SovRom ceramics factory and then of the roads repairmen at the People's Council, he had been a cheerful and lenient man, who firmly believed that evils should be put behind one, often making a gesture with his hand as though he were tossing something over his shoulder. There was also exclusive information about him, for example that from his garret room he simply and skillfully hunted pigeons, which he cooked in the oven like a maestro, with bay leaves and a white wine sauce. I had learned of this occupation of the old man by chance and in a rather abusive way, the day I climbed the dark spiral staircase at the top of which was a door. I knocked vigorously. No one hastened to open the door, and no voice bid me enter. I had pressed on the door handle like an oaf, not so much because I had promised Paulina that I would go there, as much as for Jojo, who had remained alone for a while, absorbed in the details of manicure and pedicure, meticulously brushing on her unusual olive nail varnish, obliged to inhale through the slightly open windows the perfume of the jasmine bush or the stench of the neighbors' hen coops, depending on which way the wind was blowing, waiting for the agreed doorbell signal, one long followed by three short buzzes. It was late to visit the old man and probably pointless. It was the week before the arrival of those anthropologists from Argentina, about whom everyone knew so little and from whom they were expecting so much, a kind of jury who, from between so many contradictory explanations for the mass grave, were to proclaim only one as true. And when I entered I was met neither with an empty room nor with a soundly sleeping occupant, but with a man who gazed at me, intrigued and stern, from a chair placed to one side of the window, behind a curtain. In novelistic terms, he could be described as follows: he had floury white skin; locks of hair fell over his brow, likewise white, but the color of rich butter; the pale hazel eyes defied the wrinkles at their corners; the mouth drooped to one side, betraying an old facial paralysis; a round chin protruded from between cheeks and neck; the nose was nondescript, neither snub, nor aquiline, nor sharp, nor thick, nor large, nor small—it looked like a template for cosmetic surgery. His expression inspired authority and patience, concentration, wonderment, sovereignty, largesse. Dumitru M. did not seek to conceal what he was doing and gave no explanations. He requested that I find a seat in that room sweltering under the tin roof, and that I should be silent and not hinder him. He was using a short, extendable rod, of the kind used to catch pike. On the reel there was a light-brown nylon line, at the end of which dangled a small anchor garnished with kernels of maize. From time to time he would place the tackle on the windowsill, as discreetly as possible, in a place baited with crusts of bread and a few handfuls of kernels. He would peer into a round mirror positioned on the edge of the desk so that he would not miss anything that was going on outside, while himself remaining unobserved. He chased away the sparrows and jays with a short whistle, retrieving the lure from those greedy birds full of bones and gristle, as he waited for the pigeons. Sometimes he would attempt a kind of cooing, but his vocal cords, I think (in fact, I am convinced), were devoid of any alluring virtues. The first catch occurred around twenty minutes after I arrived. There was a strong clatter of wings, a flapping at the sill: it was a plump gray ringdove, whose neck he quickly wrung. It was not until then that the old man rose and extended his hand to me, amiably, and invited me to have a cup of milky tea. He owed the habit, as he made clear from the very start, to the salons of pre-Communist days. Somewhat later, after I had asked my questions and after he had shrugged and firmly shaken his head, he caught another two pigeons. The last one, rather scrawny, with a violet-white collar, put up such a fight that it knocked over the mirror. It did not break. "Good!" he said. "It would have meant seven years bad luck . . ." And he refilled the teacups, covered the birds with a cloth soaked in vinegar and, examining on all sides the little gold anchor that had more than done its duty, he decided to replace it with a new hook. "It's not the same as with a fish's lips. They have hard beaks, the metal crumples," he explained as his fingers fumbled with the knots of the line. "Only once have I found it otherwise, when I hooked a homing pigeon. It had fragile cartilage and a stupid message in the ring on its leg: 'The mountains are high,' or something of the sort. I could not resist making it into a soup with caraway, tarragon, and cream. It turned out very sweet. I discovered the pigeon fancier a week later. It was the Pilot, as I had suspected. He was complaining to some ladies outside the post office about how his homing pigeon had vanished, and how he had been Party secretary at a number of airbases, without ever having taken off, without even having climbed into a cockpit. How glad I was!" Later, Dumitru M. interrupted a boar-hunting story from the days before nationalization and all the rest: "You keep shifting from one leg to another, young man, you're shuffling

your shoes. Are you bored? Do you want to know where the
WC is?" I pointed at his alarm clock, which was ticking on a
shelf near his shoulder, and told him that if I did not reach the
park in half an hour, at the sixth bench counting from the or-
namental lake toward the bandstand, I risked upsetting someone very much. It all became clear to him: "Ah, so that's how
it is, that's how it is. When it's a question of a woman, there is
no discussion . . ." I had risen to leave and did not refuse an in-
vitation to lunch the next day, even if I was not hurrying to the
park, but rather not to miss the sunset under the little skylight
in Auntie Paulina's house.

As I descended, above the creaking of the pinewood stairs
I heard the bolt of a door and Paraschiva, the old man's wife,
emerged in front of me, with a shawl tied around her middle,
wearing glasses for severe myopia, and holding a plate of biscuits. She knew a great deal about me, from my name to the
annoyances of my ulcer, from my profession to my inability
to give up smoking, from my desire to see the site of the archaeological dig reopened to my weakness for jazz. She listed
everything rapidly, as a courteous introduction, as though she
were uttering a few remarks about the weather. She was a creature from whom old age had not sufficiently erased an impera-
tive side.

I told her that I was in a terrible rush, that I had to run, but
she pinned me to the foot of the stairs, in order to describe the
miracle of the blade from her meat grinder. She had awoken
shortly after midnight, at the close of the fast, she had waited
until one o'clock, quarter past one, so as not to surrender to
the appetites of her stomach immediately, after weeks of ab-
stinence, and then she had tried to grind the beef intended that

evening for meatballs. However, the meat grinder got jammed at the first turn of the handle. She had dismantled it clumsily; her hands would not obey her. She had almost smashed the cup of egg yolks. She discovered that the blade was missing, although she took care to have it sharpened twice a year and immediately returned to its place. She was racking her brain, the ceiling had tilted to the left, then to the right—it had looked like a hammock seen from below, she claimed. She had refrained from measuring her blood pressure using the apparatus on the nightstand, convinced that she would read an alarming figure on the screen ("a German apparatus, electrical, from my daughter . . ."). She had turned the whole kitchen upside down, emptying the cupboards, clearing the shelves, but found nothing. As she spoke, her eyes blazed under the thick lenses; a strand from her well-kept coiffure rose on her forehead like an Apache feather. She had prayed, she had wept, and in the end she had calmed down, but without going to sleep or being capable of doing anything else. Toward morning, she had telephoned the woman whom she was expecting to arrive to do the cleaning and asked her to bring another meat grinder. It was a blue one. She had carefully attached it to the edge of the table, filled it with pieces of meat, at first with what she had recovered from inside her green grinder, and turned the handle. It moved as it should, she laughed, asked the woman how her granddaughter was doing, listened to how the little girl was learning poems about bugs and animals, how she coughed and drew houses, until a strange gnashing arose and the mechanism refused to function. She had been ready to faint, she barely caught hold of the sideboard. (Her eyes were now incan-

descent: "He smites me! He smites me for not having veered
from the holy commandments for so long! And the fast . . ."
"Who, madam?" I asked. "Your husband?" "No-o-o, eh, the
poor man! He is a sinner and stubborn, but not he, the Unclean
One . . .") She had no longer felt in a fit state for anything.
The cleaning woman was pale all of a sudden, and mute. But
how good our Lord God had been to her! From the strands of
meat pulled out of the funnel of the grinder, in the silence of
the kitchen, had emerged an object in the form of a crucifix,
stamped with the number 5. "Mr. Petrus," she whispered (and
a few tears trickling down to her lips merged into one large
drop), "do you understand? My blade was in the meat grinder
of the poor woman and the Heavenly Father sent her to me
as a messenger, to show that He has not abandoned me, that
He loves me." The sun was no longer on the point of setting,
it had completely set, and I advised her in the future to better
tighten the parts of her meat grinder.

You can deceive Eugenia Embury with an easy heart, observing that so many cats and flowers leave no room for suspi-
cion, knowing that the lethargy of the small felines and the fra-
grances of the plants bend the eyes toward the past, and not
toward the day that is already slipping away or toward times
to come. To lie to her, however, is an arbitrary abuse, not because she is a delicate person, but because the truth does not
irritate her, whatever its appearance. As a result, so as not to
commit such a sin, Jojo had to go to Bucharest, even if only
for a day, in order to sit a student exam she had missed during
the time without fruit metaphors when we did not know each

other. We had decided together that the journey was obligatory, having watched her grandmother countless times from
behind the flounced curtains of Paulina's house, whispering,
trying to compose an image of Lord Embury as close as possible to what he must have been, from snatches of descriptions,
from epistolary lines read in secret, from deductions, from the
physiognomy that the few photographs revealed to us, from
sequences imagined in the great tradition of logic, from the
material crumbs of their short conjugal life, which amounted
to a hot-water bottle made of natural rubber, a dozen Japanese
fans, a few pipes and atlases, a small revolver skillfully hidden
away from secret police searches, and a champagne glass. In
a state of denial, we kept putting off the problem of the fac-
ulty examination, regularly telephoning the secretariat, until it
became clear that the meteorology professor was only to be
found one more Wednesday and would afterward disappear to
an international congress.

Jojo was the keeper of all the secrets of the Embury couple. She had read the letters, she had seen the photographs, and
she had discovered the pistol beneath the false bottom of the
mailbox on the front of the house, a place where the militiamen
and secret police had never looked, although inside the house
they used to turn everything upside down. And at sunset, only
Jojo had that fantastic power over colors, transforming red into
green, then into ultramarine and mauve, simply by baring her
shoulders and breasts. I had unreservedly accepted the invita-
tion to lunch from Dumitru M. because it coincided with that
Wednesday, and after Jojo left at dawn (before it became light,
so as not to be seen from the windows round about and not to

meet any acquaintances on the way to the station), I snoozed
for a while in a hot bath, using her bath salts and bubbles.
Later, when it was barely half past eight, I realized something
unusual: I was continually looking at the clock. Not one of the
books on the nightstand tempted me. Reviewing the observations in my notebook was useless. At one point I turned on the
radio, and quickly turned it off. I put some clothes in water to
soak, but did not get around to washing them. I went out into
the yard with a rug. The sun was burning quite brightly and
after scorching my back for a little while, it made me at last
want something: a cold shower. In the cupboard I had plenty
of food, but I did not touch it, so as to arouse my hunger as
much as possible before experiencing the culinary abilities of
the oldest man in town. I set off for his house at eleven o'clock,
not the direct way, because I would have arrived in a few minutes, but taking a long detour through the streets and lanes
that climbed toward the old fire station, a place from which, if
you sat with your back to the Prussian-style buildings and the
town spread out below them, the only thing that you saw were
mountains. Above the woods floated a summer mist. It rose
over the valleys and steep slopes, though not very far, it did
not reach the rocks and boulders, it left untouched that patch
beneath the southern slope that only the trained eye could distinguish. However, toponomy is a curious science, hostile to
the present, faithful to the equivocal past, ready to accept as
gospel doubtful collective memories and dismiss out of hand
what can be seen or touched. The distant patch, a clearing in
which the stones of a small structure lay piled among the undergrowth, was called the Finn's cabin, and brought to mind

that morning when Jojo had tossed her clothes onto the grass and unbuckled my belt, laughing.

In spite of my walk, Paraschiva M. took care that I should not arrive too early for lunch. She again barred my way at the foot of the stairs, this time with her hair well pinned back, offering no biscuits, telling me that whoever scoffs at a divine miracle is an ignoramus or a pagan. I agreed with her ("a miracle is a miracle, madam," I found myself quoting Auntie Paulina), but I did not conceal from her that I had a different opinion about the so-called miracle. And this is what I believed: the blade of the meat grinder had not been attached properly, it had come loose and upset the mechanism, she had not noticed it when she emptied the funnel, and she had put it into some pan or other along with the meat ("this happens with small objects," I added, "especially when such severe myopia is involved and one is in such a state that the ceiling sways like a hammock"), she had then searched for it in vain, and the cleaning woman, being in a hurry ("the poor woman probably wanted to get it over with as quickly as possible," I explained), had stuffed it into the other grinder along with the pieces of meat, with the onions and breadcrumbs. "An ignoramus or a pagan!" she repeated with upraised forefinger. She slammed the door and noisily drew the bolt. I climbed the pinewood stairs, because the old man was waiting for me above, coughing to make his presence heard, dressed in a white shirt and black velvet waistcoat.

And lunch was amazing! The taste. The taste of the pigeons. Before which all else paled: the garb of the host, the porcelain plates with undulated edges, the rigorous distances between glasses, the cutlery with its Austrian hallmark, the streak of light on the silver lid of the platter and then the liquid beneath, also gleaming, covering the bronze curves of the game hunted the day before. The setting of that lunch stirred feelings, it conquered, it prepared for the joy of the taste buds; just as in childhood, in a house loyal to fried potatoes, my culinary fantasies would have been inconceivable in the absence of the illustrations in the cookbook, which yielded to touch, even kisses: a miniature indulgence, with its vividly colored photographs of steaks, soufflés, salads and puddings, most sprinkled with herbs and spices, some set in aspic, and just as splendid were the tarts, cakes, and charlottes dusted with confectioner's sugar, drizzled with syrup, on which were resplendent fresh or preserved fruits. As for Dumitru M., he was an artist of gastronomy, who had ennobled a rousing combination: roast pigeon in white wine sauce. I was grateful to him, as I sat smoking, listening, sipping an almond-flavored German digestif.

SCENE 1: *He dabs his lips with a napkin. He makes a gesture over his shoulder, there is a white wall upon which he will give an imaginary projection of events from the war.*

"How much I envied the field mice! It was not hard to spot them in that stunted grass, more couch grass than anything else. They would be scrabbling for roots, ripping out the spines of thistle heads to get to the kernel. I would watch a hamster circling the puddles before venturing to drink. And how it would drink! Rapidly, its tongue no bigger than a quarter of a fingernail. I managed to observe the tongue from time to time through the binoculars: minuscule, not pink, whitish, without any connection to the ruddy fur. I would see the hamster van-

ishing in one place and reappearing in another, its nose ready
to receive whatever was borne on the wind: the scent of chamomile, of latrines, of corpses, of brackish stews from the field
kitchens. I used to like it when it sat up on its hind paws, heed-
ful of noises and shadows. It would sometimes hap that this in-
quisitive gesture would be its last, because there would be some
swine in the trench who pulled the trigger, out of an aversion
to all rodents, or to relieve the boredom, or to win some bet
with his friends. In such situations, the hamster was neither
cited for a medal, nor decorated postmortem. But if the bullet
missed, the hamster would fill the tunnels with young. It would
get off at will. Something which was impossible for us. On the
other hand, to us were forthcoming plenty of honors, including monuments, with their inexplicable predilection for squares
and railway stations, massive monuments, always with room
for long lists of names. And then there was the compassion of
the ladies, who adored heroes. They lit candles after Sunday
mass and on High Holidays. When I say that I envied the field
mice, I really did envy them: that is how I came to lay my
hands on an unwashed peasant woman, in a barn, after three
higher-ranking officers. She had a sour smell like an over-
worked mare, she was slatternly, with watery eyes, and she
kept squashing her tits, as though she were squeezing lemons.
That night I drained a bottle of plum brandy by myself. There
must have been two or three pints. I wept and I dreamed of
girls with hats and parasols, with adorably painted lips and
cheeks, the girls who moved on the stage as if made of rubber.
In the morning, they told me that I had performed a long
French cancan number and that I had threatened with my pistol
all those who tried to stop me. Hunched on the hood of a truck,

tirelessly kicking my legs, lifting up the skirts of my greatcoat, I had paid homage to those young dancing girls, actresses, and chanteuses who were so far away, in a vanished world, which some lied would be reborn. I had been applauded by the troops, but also, from somewhere in the night, by those different uniforms, with a star on their caps, who had shown that they too knew how to whoop and laugh. I had not been disturbed by a single gunshot, which meant that all had gone well for the hamsters. And I had paid homage to the girls for their gaiety. For the smutty laugh that did not cease until we entered the large hall of my house, where they were overcome by pallor. They fearfully examined the paintings, the pieces of porcelain, and the candelabra, they trod the carpet as if it were the hob of an oven, they looked the valet up and down and allowed themselves to be studied in their turn, in a fit of mutual curiosity. They deserved to be pinched on the chin or the earlobe, but the boy who opened the salon doors, invited them inside, put some music on the gramophone, at a low volume, poured them liqueurs, and invited them to sink into the armchairs deserved a kick in the behind, because he did not understand that you can look at someone without ogling. I kept them in clover; I spoiled them like queens. I was the master. And so I remained for a long time, until Paraschiva made her appearance, in the epoch when the Maginot Line, in spite of its age and the uninterrupted eulogies, still looked invincible and had not lost its status as a fashionable subject. The French inspired strength, and I could not manage to distinguish between the four sisters who had lately arrived on my street. I used to meet them out walking, at the skating rink, at the summer theaters: mellow, coquettish, inseparable, children blushing from the cold, the heat, the dust, the pollen, perhaps it was a family trait that always made them radiate freshness or emotion. I would raise my hat politely, an obligatory salute. Her I did not notice until one evening, in my office, as I was dozing off by the stove, watching the raindrops playing on the panes of the street lamps. Across the road there was a circular window, a kind of porthole emerging for the first time from beneath the protection of drapes, and Paraschiva, with hair undone, black, long as her hips, was pacing somnolently through the room. She was covered by a transparent nightshirt, and through the milky veil could be distinguished a virgin's body that had very well understood what was happening to it and what was to come. She must have been before a mirror, preoccupied with each detail reproduced by the silvered glass. She would lean forward and comb her hair to her knees, then her shoulders would be bared, she would arch her back and so many things occurred, the tips of her locks would cover her ankles, a patch would appear beneath her belly, slightly bulging, like a pincushion, two little hummocks with light-brown tufts would grow on her chest. My pipe had gone out without my noticing, proof that Dutch tobacco was not my main passion. Her face toward me, Paraschiva undid her buttons and allowed the vaporous vestment to slide down. The raindrops had merged into a thick web on the round windowpane. I bit on the cherry wood, the pipe creaked between my teeth and then cracked, but the slender body did not reveal its nakedness. From beneath the fine fabric of raindrops there appeared a blue dress, of thick material, through which not one single thread of light could pass. An austere dress, which at once lent her face the bearing of a governess of the Austrian school: the rigid neck and clenched lips, the regally raised chin, the hands joined in the region where the stomach passes via the pylorus into the duodenum. The light bulb in her room soon went out, the house became gloomy, and the outline of the window was lost in the dark. The scene of voyeurism had come to an end, the first, that which heralds the pleasure. I remained standing long after midnight, next to the stove. I had never believed in illusions, even less so in magic. Outside, it was raining heavily. The roofs rattled under the huge raindrops. On the following evenings I did not go out. The sky was serene, glassy, such as it is only in winter, and the performance was repeated, always at the same hour: a maddening, captivating dance. The young woman was becoming more and more accustomed to her own shapes and with the role in which the celestial director had cast her. She would rustle, she would flutter, her svelte thighs would rub against the translucent silk—Paraschiva was made of marble! After that, with regularity, the miraculous nightshirt would gently be abandoned, and that sober, insufferable frock would make its appearance. We married in February, during a bracing frost, not five months after the destruction of my cherry wood pipe. But before the wedding, I made a host of visits to that shiplike house, the fruit of the architect's nautical inclinations or perhaps of a longed-for cruise. The young lady played the piano, tenaciously. She would play a few ballads while her father, a diligent functionary of the legal system, would croon the verses. The little concerts delighted Paraschiva's sisters, for they could busy themselves in peace with the truffles, raisin biscuits, and glazed walnuts. They would munch discreetly, so as to permit the notes and words to resound. Except that Eleanor, an aunt never absent at such gatherings, would sometimes forget the solemnity of the moment, and, captivated by the confectionery, begin to chomp noisily. She would straightaway receive a nudge from the mother, her first cousin, look around her with astonishment, and settle her hands in her lap. In resignation. Then she would scrutinize the complicated pattern of the wallpaper, the sinuous lines, overlaid with regular geometric figures, in a blend of green and mustard yellow. I found out from a businessman, a customer of my factory, that when she was forty pounds lighter she had been engaged to the aviation pioneer Aurel Vlaicu. And I felt sorry for the poor aviator. Those days, if he hadn't already been smashed to smithereens crossing the Carpathians, I would have willingly built him a hundred airplanes. From my own pocket. Later, however, after two or three weeks of marriage, I lost that urge. Paraschiva had refused to share a bedroom, on the first night citing a migraine, on the following three putting her indisposition down to nausea, and afterward giving me to understand, in the language of good breeding, that she had to put up with a tremendous, unprecedented menstruation, and finally giving no more explanations. I avoided my old habits, because the lady was not at all impressed by the perfume of liqueurs or by the novelty of gramophone disks. At least I saved some money. I was to know her caresses later, before they sent me to the front. "They are all leaving for their country," she whispered in my ear after a dinner of veal cutlet and cauliflower au gratin. She took me by the hand and led me to the still immaculate nuptial bed. We climbed the stairs on tiptoe, she with her finger to her lips, as though someone might have surprised us, I as obedient as a little dog, a poodle or a terrier. She managed without lighting any lamp. She found the door, the handle, the bedspread over the sheets. She passed them all and pulled me down on top of her, as open as a shellfish. "These are not times for love," she told me toward morning, wrapped in sheets, running her fingers over my chest. She was made of marble! Barely had I begun to number the journeys from the dining room to that magical chamber on the upper floor, when all at once I discovered fear, the sickly scent of blood, fat lice from which it was possible to melt down an acceptable boot polish, scabies, the taste of moldy bread, the metallic chill of the guns—if not affectionate then at least life-saving—the cold, the damp, the concern for one's own skin before the tumult of victory and the aims of the homeland, the lack of any notion of an umbrella when it started or when it wouldn't stop raining, admiration for the field mice, always in search of food over those fallow fields. And she did not heed her own words: to her the times proved ideal for love. It was not even a case of some quartermaster or a handsome young man with a noncombatant's certificate. But of Jesus Christ."

SCENE 2: *The slightly dry wine goes well with the afternoon warmth. To the left of the old man there is a studded trunk. He is about to lift its lid, enough to let the stagnant air of peacetime escape.*

"From up high, people look like insects. In winter, against the expanse of snow, as they jerkily walk around, they look like cockroaches crawling over the rough surface of a freshly whitewashed ceiling. Whenever the cold overcame me, and this used to happen quickly, however many sweaters, long johns, and pairs of socks I wore, I would feel the urge to crush them. After a while, the feeling would pass. I would need two or three shots of brandy to start feeling mercy, even if in the cabin of the crane my hands were beginning to ice to the iron levers, freezing solid. I gazed at how they gathered around fires and stamped their feet, how they gesticulated when they argued, how they kept pulling their fur hats over their ears and how they gave each other cigarettes, without being sure who was smoking and who was not, because the smoke would be mixed up with the steam of their breath. They were earning crumbs on the building sites of SovRom. In fact, they were not earning it, God no! It was given away to them by the Communists, those large-hearted lads, who might as well have registered them in the inventories of the agricultural cooperatives, along with the horses and cattle. In my case they didn't put their heart into it . . . They taught me a trade. A grown man, after they had taken away my houses, factory, vineyard, paintings, jewels, and money, they made me a crane operator. And they fired a bullet into the head of Pascal, a magnificent Irish setter, a prince, as he was pressing up against the knees of my wife on the couch. He stretched out further than usual, a trickle of blood emerged from under his ear and found its way down to his chest, to his tuft of white fur, his eyes remained half-closed, expressing something that the Communists will never be able to understand. Paraschiva screamed, except it wasn't so much a scream as a devastation, a sound that did not belong to the vo-cal cords, but they laughed and continued to rummage through the bookcase, one of them shouted: "What is it, milady, couldn't you tell he was going to bite you?!" At minus nine or fourteen or twenty degrees, my memory used to contract hypothermia, many things no longer mattered. I could remember only the mink coat. I had come home by hackney carriage, after lunch, it was immediately after Saint Mary Magdalene's Day, and at the gate I bumped into a weedy individual, with a number of teeth missing, his hair was slicked back with lard, certainly not with brilliantine. He was on his way out carrying a bundle of clothes, he hesitated, he didn't know whether to go round me or to make a run for it, he kept saying that the mistress is very charitable. And so she was. In his arms I recognized the mink coat, a few suits, some silk pajamas with the buttons missing, and a ski jacket. I espied Paraschiva in the doorway, smiling, trying to fend off the heat with a fan. I didn't use my stick, or my fist, I took out my wallet and paid the coachman for two trips, the one just taken and another in advance, then I helped the leech climb up and, with my back turned on my wife, I cursed the mother that bore him. But during a frost like that, without fail I would long for the coat. Especially since the Canadian boots, which nobody had thought of nationalizing, were losing their insulating properties. My feet used to turn to blocks of ice, my kidneys hurt worse and worse, until at some point in January, toward the end of the month, I could no longer hold it in and I pissed from the height of the crane cabin. The jet and the stain on the ground, on the snow more than thirty feet below me, were not yellowish but reddish, a strawberry color. A good thing I had the brandy. Consumed in serious quantities, it helped me to forget, to endure for a few more days. It was made from sorb-apples and I used to buy it from a Gypsy with a lisp, an accordionist who did not want money in exchange, but gramophone records. In any case, while I was working as a crane driver I blew my entire collection. It had once numbered more than six hundred disks. I wasn't very sorry, because in the hospital you're overcome by the heat. They had given me a frayed and dirty blanket, but the stove guzzled so much wood that at night I would dream I was at the public baths, in the sauna. On top of everything else, whenever the fire was lit, the smoke would seep through the cracks in the tiles of the stove and invade the ward, imparting a little intimacy. The figures in the other beds did not become invisible, but they receded, dissolved, ended up indistinguishable, thank God, from the décor. Only the voices remained, with all kinds of pitches and inflexions, infinite discussions about the war, vegetables, liver attacks, and women, surpassing the effects of any medication. The reason was simple: radio plays have always lulled me to sleep. There was one voice I really liked, Ghitza's, because if it hadn't been for him, the cold would have taken control of the huge room in which we languished, the same as it had in the rest of the hospital. It wasn't the fault of Ghitza, an upholsterer with renal insufficiency, if his brother was a major in the Securitate, on the other hand the coal took this fact into account and heaped itself into our stove. Paraschiva didn't visit me until March, convinced that the time had come to administer the last rights. She was dressed in black, from her shoes to her cashmere shawl, while, even under the circumstances, her face gleamed like marble. I knew that my wife, when traveling, didn't like voluminous baggage, and her premature display of grief didn't upset me. She was accompanied by a young priest, who was blond, not at all talkative, and, from all appearances, undergoing a prolonged fast. He studied me compassionately, no doubt wondering what had become of the part of me that had left this world. They were pleasant enough, but I sent them away after only a minute. Because they hadn't brought me flowers. No snowdrops, no freesias, not even any immortelles.

They left in silence, piously, as is fitting when one withdraws from the cemetery after lighting a candle in the family vault. Sighing, Paraschiva closed the door as softly as she had opened it, she ought to have intoned Amen in the doorway. As for my urine, it regained its original clarity some time around the middle of April. It was a Wednesday when the red blood cells obediently made their way back into my veins and arteries, into the capillaries ramified throughout my tissues. The young doctor emphatically wiped the lenses of his spectacles and for a good few minutes examined in amazement the liquid collected in the jar. I imitated him countless times in the week that followed, in the toilet, in the filthy cubicle where I would admire the yellowish hues delicately dispersed over the faience like lemonade. I had been dispossessed of a kidney, but it was a reasonable loss as long as the cherry trees in the hospital courtyard had burst into white, myriad, tiny flowers, fragile as butterflies. And sprouting grass surrounded the building behind the wards, lending it a more bearable aspect. In a sunny, cheerful setting, perhaps Ghitza's departure in a coffin would have looked different. In the first place, all of us, gathered at the windows of the ward, wouldn't have looked on the morgue as such a repellent building, nor would we have kept such a grim silence. And, his relatives, sheltering under umbrellas and raincoats, careful not to sink up to their knees in the mud, might have been able to imagine at least for a moment the verdant place the priest had mentioned. I came out of the hospital in the spring. With two carrier bags in my hands, my retirement certificate in my pocket, and a pair of worn-out boots on my feet. I was informed that my Canadian boots had gone astray in the storeroom. The young doctor came running up behind me at the end of the central avenue, near the gates, his pallor had disappeared due to the exertion and two purple spots pigmented his cheeks. He led me by the arm into the street, maintaining that he owed me a lot. I replied that it was I who remained in his debt, but that I couldn't repay him at just that moment. He smiled. Poor chap! I found out later that he committed suicide while laboring on the Black Sea–Danube Canal, in his fifth year of detention. He had hanged himself with a rope woven from scraps of prison uniform, in the laundry room. Since I had no business anywhere else, it was back here in the village that I rediscovered how kindhearted the Communists were. Eleven children, I counted them, were running riot in the small apple orchard, the balcony on the upper floor was overrun with washing hung out to dry, and on the ground floor, on the terrace, some women were peeling beans, prattling, with a hatching-hen and a brood of chicks at their feet. One of them advised me to be thankful, another, older, fat, asked me why the hell I hadn't died, because her son was getting married and he had his eye on my room. I wasn't sure whether she was joking or not, but what was certain was that five families had moved into the house, while the People's Council tolerated us, for a rent, in the garret. In this room. Into which had been heaped so many things. I recognized an armchair from the old library, a cupboard, the dressing table less its mirror, the grandfather clock, a few icons. It hadn't been aired for a long time and the dust had settled like a sad film, even the envelope that was waiting for me on a shelf had to be blown and shaken before I opened it. Paraschiva, in violet ink, informed me that she had elected to take the veil. She asked me not to disturb her and advised me not to demolish the north wall of the cellar. She had already seen to it herself. Such are the times, she wrote, and the cool of evening caused me to put back on the coat I had hung on a nail. If she had not donated the pearl necklace, she added, the mother superior would not have accepted her into the monastery."

SCENE 3: *Twirled between fingers, the stem of the empty glass. It seems to him that the smoke from a bonfire of leaves is coming through the window, a sign of the time that was and that is to come.*

"We did not exchange a word for six years. Before, I used to have my cupboard downstairs, in the hall. I kept it locked, as a riposte, because she had been the first to keep her provisions under lock and key. When I came down, I would open it with the little key, take what I needed from inside, and go to cook and eat in the kitchen. She would eavesdrop at her door. She would hear the tap of my stick and my receding steps, the sound of the dishes and the cutlery, the water flowing from the faucet, she knew when she could come out and rummage and choose what she liked from my cupboard. As a rule, she stole sweets and fruit, cheese very rarely. One day, I imitated those sounds: I tapped with my stick on the floor and trod with my slippers on the spot, more and more quietly. I surprised her after she had emerged from her room and was filling her teacup from the honey pot. When she saw me, she cried out softly and lifted her hands. The honey spilled on her dress and sweater, the handle of the cup chipped, and the pot smashed into pieces. I laughed. Since then she has never even said hello to me. What did she tell you? That you are an ignoramus and a pagan? Don't be annoyed with Paraschiva."

CHAPTER SIX

T HE NUMBER 2 CAN sometimes be the beginning, the origin, although, in the formal order of the numbers, *1* is still to be found in its own place. In such situations, *1* appears as a consequence, it has a meaning only if *2* exists. And this paradox of mathematics, a fruit of mystic intuition rather than of Cartesian deductions, was the rule whereby Gherghe (later Onufrie) greeted the Virgin's descents from the azure of the firmament. Properly speaking, if there had been no second apparition of the Holy Mother in his life, the first would have passed unseen; it would have been a squandered miracle. It was necessary for Her to be incarnated, with a gentle but authoritative mien, at the mouth of a mineshaft, on Saturday, May 16, at the very exit from the prisoner's tunnel, in order to banish his ignorance and fathom the mystery of a prior encounter. Onufrie in his unique way hallows that day, each passing year adding a new knife notch to his right forefinger, precisely because the dazzling present of that day illumined his past and, to a great extent, his future. In the weeks after his escape, he lived like a wild animal, hiding by day in gullies and thickets, moving by night only when the moonlight was faint, avoiding villages and towns, even sheepfolds and shacks in orchards and hayfields, keeping far from beaten tracks, roads, and railway lines, crossing rivers and lakes straight through the water, in desolate spots, never over bridges, shunning people, whether they wore a uniform or not. He was in no hurry to reach any particular place at any precise time. He was a fugitive satisfied with his immediate fate and with the truth lately revealed to him. Early summer spared him from the cold; it was the time of ramson, of balm mint, of poor man's asparagus, and of the black fungi that grow on beech and plane trees, and so he did not endure hunger; he rediscovered the senses and instincts of an abandoned child that had learned to fend for itself, and over him, strengthening him, settled the feeling of a blessing received from on high. Had someone picked up his trail, collecting the tufts of bluish-black hair lopped and abandoned every four hours, his route, one that was atypical and aleatory in the first place because it had a point of departure but no destination, would have resembled, on being transposed onto a map, the scribble of a spoiled little girl, in which the lines intersect—now pointy, now curved—move to the right only to come back to the left, rise and fall higgledy-piggledy. That peregrination, in which time had no measure, did, however, allow him to discover something other than new regions of the country. His joy and affection, fresh as they were, had first of all given birth to the question of whether somehow, before memory first established itself, this saving descent of Mary had been preceded by another. He was fearful of the sin of pride and whispered hundreds of prayers, falling to his knees wherever this fear overcame him, on grass and brushwood, on the mud of ploughed fields or on the soft moss of the forest, on molehills or in the mire. The question slowly, slowly transformed into an opinion, but proof was lacking, and so he had to seek arguments. And, one cloudless night, he resorted to *reductio ad absurdum.* He had no knowledge of this method, but as a diligent pupil of the Lord he presupposed that the Mother of God had never intervened in his life until he arrived at the labor camp. And, imagining things to be thus, untouched by Providence, what would have happened? All of a sudden he realized, as he was lying in an alder copse, with pale stars strewn overhead, with one cheek nacreous, the other tenebrous, that he would have died. He would have perished, scorched by the sun on a bed of branches, struggling to free himself from the white swaddling clothes in which his true mother had swathed him, bawling until he had no more strength to move his enfolded little arms and legs. But he had lived . . . was that not proof that the Holy Mother had set foot there, on the shingle bank of the river, where Stanca (whose name, along with her face and deeds, could not have been strange to Her) had abandoned him? He leapt from his nest without noticing the tomtit and the bee-eater that started and took flight. He burst through the thorny foliage, he ran up a clayey slope, then along the crest of a hill, as if pursued by the moonbeams, shouting at the top of his voice, not words, but long singing vowels. Sometimes he tripped and fell, but he got up and kept on running. He ran and shouted until the outlines of things—trees, hills, vineyards, a sleeping hamlet, the jagged line of the horizon, a mill—began to whirl around him, just as on that whirligig at the fair he had gone to with old biddy Vutza long ago, where he had learnt that he would be left in peace if he went around with his head covered. And he collapsed. On one shoulder, in a faint, on top of some henbane stalks. He came to himself shivering, his face scratched and dirty. His tears mingled with the dust and the crumbled soil on his eyelids and cheekbones. He had wounded his chin and in the grazed, bloody skin shone grit. He did not rise. He curled up like a wet dog. He sobbed, now knowing that the Mother of God must have examined the expanses up and down the river to convince Herself that no human foot ever trod there. She must have taken him in Her arms and cradled him for a while, have rid him of his diaper and the filth of his bottom, have washed him in the lukewarm water that pooled near the bank, for She would not have plunged him into the icy stream. Perhaps She had wiped him and clothed him with a scrap torn from Her shirt or Her skirt and, moved by his whimpers, given him Her dug. The same dug from which Her Son once sucked, or the other? Had he heard a lullaby once heard by Him, or another one? Had the thigh of Stanca's newborn son, the left one, been milky, translucent, and rosy like that of the Holy Infant, which he had pricked with the tip of his scissors? Gherghe was melted and at the same time frightened by the boldness of what he was imagining and discovering. And his tears were different from those other tears shed at Neamtz Monastery, though the latter, in their steadfastness and abundance, had caused one corner of the mat before the holy icon to molder, the holy icon he had first pricked and then venerated. He fell asleep weeping, with his knees pressed to his chest, clasped between his elbows, looking much smaller than he had come to be. He awoke immediately after the dew had fallen, so that he found other drops on his brow and clothes. Out of thirst, with a leaf for a scoop he gathered droplets from the blades of grass. Instead of that question that had been gnawing at him day after day (when eating, he would sometimes stop chewing and remained for seconds, even whole minutes, with his mouth open and the morsel unswallowed; he would stop ever more frequently in the middle of a prayer, losing the thread of the words and obliged to start all over again from the beginning), a question that had imperceptibly transformed into an opinion (following him everywhere, in his diurnal shelters or his journeys in darkness), instead of both of these, that is, instead of the question and the opinion that had accompanied his last twilight, in fact all his many evenings before and after Midsummer's Day, there had arisen overnight the conviction that the Holy Mother had once before taken care of him, there on the bank of the river, for many hours, until She saw in the distance another woman, a mortal woman, who was to be his adoptive mother. The scratches on his cheek stung him, the grit in his chin had been enveloped by a swelling as big as a plum, with a scarlet crust, his ankle ached dully—he must have trodden crookedly as he ran or twisted it in one of his falls. How many things had happened, and he had not felt them! The sharp branches that had lashed his face, the steep slope of the hill, the cough that had now and then interrupted his shouts, his heartbeats exceedingly happy, but wracked by his frantic flight, the blows, the earth that he had gnashed between his teeth, the risk of being seen by malicious persons and of being caught. The time had come to cut the tuft on his crown and he was startled as never before when he pulled from his pocket the scissors. He clenched them in his palm, for a moment he wanted to throw them away, but he didn't.

A conviction is no longer a presupposition, nor a torment in itself. As a rule, it does not bring to a close a period of sleeplessness in order to bring repose and reverie, but rather provokes other presuppositions and torments. And Gherghe now learned with astonishment how many new doubts, fears, and illusions were born of a freshly discovered fact. For instance, he would say to himself, in fright, that the details he had imagined, such as that first effort of the Virgin not to let him perish, might have been blasphemous aberrations of his mind. That this first descent had genuinely taken place was beyond doubt, but was the way in which he pictured the miracle not a sin? On what grounds had he come to believe that the Holy Mother had unswaddled him and wiped his dirty bottom? What need was there for Her to sacrifice Her vestments and, above all (oh, Lord, this required of him a black fast), why would She allow his lips to touch and to possess Her breast? Why would Her lips have hummed him a lullaby? In the end, he entered a thicket of hypotheses and delusions. He had tolerated better than other men the depths of the copper mine and the prison above: the elevator-cage, the narrow and miry tunnels, the feeble light of the lamps, the rusty rock that they broke up with their picks, the venom of the guards, the spectacle of human nature and behavior in prison uniform, which joined wailing and stubbornness, denunciations, pettiness, crawling, camaraderie, courteousness, and mercy. But the Immaculate Virgin had decided to spare him. It was, it goes without saying, an argument in support of the other divine descent, the first, because there is a great difference between difficult and grave, and if She had got him out of the labor camp, out of a difficult situation, then how much more so must She have assisted in a grave situation, on the riverbank, when he would have perished unnamed and unbaptized. And there was something else. Had not death somehow been lurking in the mine too, without him suspecting it? Maybe he was to have been caught under a caved-in roof or to have fallen down a shaft. Maybe one of the guards, sick of threatening and swearing, was to have started playing with his pistol and even to have pulled the trigger . . . And the Mother of God, whose gaze never slumbers and comprehends all, not only that which has been or is, but also that which is to come, hastened to wrest him from the path of the hideous form that threatened with its scythe. He found the idea pleasing, it was like honey, but did it not once more betray an immeasurable vanity? He then understood, after a late sunset, as sunsets still are at the beginning of July, gathering wild strawberries at the threshold of darkness, that his judgment had reached a deceptive point. It was as if he found himself at a crossroads, wondering which way to go, powerless to choose, until he climbed to the top of a tall tree, an oak or poplar, and observed in astonishment that the road to the left was neither longer nor harder than the one that led to the right and that both lead to the same place. However things stood, the consequence was one and the same: the Virgin Mary had for a second time abandoned the tranquility and verdure of the heavens to make sure that he remained in earthly life. She had done so with a purpose, with a plan, choosing him from among many, a tool in Her fashioning hands. He crushed the wild strawberries with the tip of his tongue, against the roof of his mouth, in the hollows of his cheeks, at the back of his teeth. He swallowed the bittersweet juice and only later the pulp. And he, Onufrie, knew he was incapable of penetrating the mystery of the Mother of the Holy Child. Having discovered what he had discovered, he no longer ran blindly up slopes or over summits, although there were plenty in that passage through the mountains, nor did he cry out or whoop, so that his crazy echo would resound. He went on all fours through the pitch blackness, slowly, feeling the grasses with all ten fingers, seeking and gathering in his fist what he thought were small fruits of the forest, chewing and swallowing the tiny leaves, stones, ants, petals, crunchy beetles, which, had he examined them by the light of day, he would have found to be green as fluorine (he had picked up so much at the mine—the names and glints of minerals), the taste had seemed to him bittersweet toward sunrise, and his duty seemed to be to remove himself far from sin, to survive by his own powers, with foresight, in order not to force Her to defend him from dangers, and to wait patiently for Her sign and Her final descent, the third, when She would show him Her succor and faith and entrust him with Her mission. At one point, a cold, damp wind had stirred up along the line of the valley, foretelling rain or perhaps only dawn, and he had grown cold and leaned against the trunk of a fir tree, on the leeward side, remembering with a kind of wonder that the previous day, before picking the first wild strawberries, he had been ready to continue his journey through a new night. How long he had hiked! Seven, almost eight, weeks, increasing not so much the distance from the men in uniform as the time that separated him from their world. And now that had come to a close. His body was sleepy, and his arms, legs, chest, and stomach were dozing at will, allowing all kinds of thoughts to come and go before the sun appeared, as it was still awakening the milky swathe above the forest. Among these thoughts there was a story concerning Father Radifir, whispered into his ear in a tunnel of the mine by Brother Arhip, whom the guards called Buluie Vasile. The reverend abbot, who had once asked him not to throw away the tufts cropped from his crown, but to collect them in a sack and to bring them to him on the first day of each month had had a contract with a Jewish wigmaker from Jassy, who sold his goods in Bonn and Marseille. A short while later, the rays of the sun nipped Onufrie's eyes, as though they had stood in salt overnight.

There, apart from the dead kid of a black goat found among the rocks from whose pelt he made himself a cap, he did not profit from the gifts of any animal, either by shearing it, milking it, cooking its flesh, or in any other way. At the beginning of autumn, he fashioned himself spindles and everything else needed to transform the bluish-black tufts into yarn, and from the ribs of the kid, left in the shade and then in a fast-flowing stream, to wash them well, he had made knitting needles, with which in time (and how long a time!) he braided gloves, vests, a scarf, socks, a blanket, two sweaters, and even a wall hanging for his cave, on which he wrote the Creed using an infusion of gentian. To tell the truth, even his underwear was made from the hair that continually grew from his crown. He might, over the course of so many years, have given up long johns, but he had once managed to read, after he had learned his letters and their interrelations, *The Rule of Our Venerable Father Pachomius the Great,* as it had been translated at Dobrusha Monastery in 1929, and in it the text of Theophanes the Recluse. And he remembered firstly from the book: "Woe unto him who, abandoning the world in order to sanctify the Lord Jesus Christ, doth not live in accordance with the vows made to Him!" And then that same Theophanes had dressed in coarse hair clothing, girding himself above, in order to cool the fires of the male body.

There, among the rocks where no one climbed, not even
the shepherds with their sheep, nor the men in uniform, nor
travelers attracted by unknown landscapes, Onufrie, just as he
had escaped from the labor camp, with no rucksack on his back
and no bundle on his shoulder, lacked many things, but above
all the Bible, for although he had concealed one in the oakum
of his mattress in the prison dormitory, a small one, with letters
the size of fleas, it had not entered his head to carry one about
his person or in his hand. And he made up his mind to recom-
pose that which his memory carried, with the tip of a hawk's
feather, using bilberry juice for ink and for paper spruce bark,
which he carefully pressed in the morning and stacked up like
timber to dry. It might be said that in the sixteen years he spent
there, a gospel according to Onufrie was published, a bizarre
text, abounding in scenes and references to the Holy Virgin, in
reality a heap, in fact many heaps, dozens, many cubic feet (it
was lucky that he had taken shelter in a capacious cave) of
wooden strips, pieces of bark shriveled and cracked with age,
and inscribed on them an unprecedented version of the Holy
Scriptures. This operation, the effort of remembrance, of cre-
ation, of preparing the writing materials and the writing itself,
filled a huge portion of Onufrie's time, alongside foraging and
repose, meditation, contemplation of the world below from
above, taking care not to leave any signs of survival in those
places, the fascination of lifting up the eyes and discovering
something even higher, and fervent waiting for the third descent of the Immaculate Virgin, Who was to entrust him with
Her plan and Her will. Onufrie was alone, hearing only the
patter of the rain, the whispering, whistling, or moaning of the

wind on the peaks, the fall of snowflakes and leaves, the flight, cheeping, and footsteps of birds, the small, gray, timorous birds of the rocks, the large, also gray, fearless birds of prey, floating above the chasms and the mists. There was water from God, from transient or perennial springs, from torrents or from rocky millraces filled with meltwater, water always good for drinking, even if it had different tastes. He had planted nine wild lilac bushes, in the form of a cross, five in a line toward the west and two to the right and left, not by his shelter, but farther away, so as not to reveal a mortal hand and arouse curiosity. When they all flowered, and they flowered seventeen times, he believed that the Mother of God would approach and delight Her nostrils with the faint perfume and rub Her cheeks with the tiny petals. He spoke to Her, telling Her his dreams or old happenings from the village in which he had grown up, from the towns through which he had passed, from the monastery, from the labor camp. He often thanked Her for Her first and for Her second descents. He assailed Her with hopes and suppositions. Sometimes it seemed to him that the clouds were gathering into the form of a woman's face, resembling Hers, and on clear nights, staring up at the firmament, he discovered clusters of stars that copied Her features. He had to be prepared in soul and in body for what was to come, and so he lent harshness to his fasting and often confessed, with himself as his own confessor, begging forgiveness in the first place for the boldness of confessing and shriving at the same time and afterward for the rest of his deeds. The candle for confessional and those for mass in his cave before the icon screen that he had painted during the first winter were made of wasp's wax collected laboriously from tree hollows, a small amount at a time, by smoking out the nests and putting up with the merciless stings. The other candles he manufactured from resin, melting it over a fire and then pouring it into slender, straight elderberry stalks, scooped of pith, into which he would slowly, slowly insert a wick made of fibers from the twill of his former prison uniform. As regards communion, in the absence of grapes he had learned to make wine from blackberries. But he did not permit himself to take Holy Communion as soon as he had confessed; he punished himself, with severity, like a monk finding out new sins at every step and seeking new steps to penitence. Once, Onufrie commanded himself to make one hundred genuflections daily for twenty-one days, because he had spoken to a bear during the fast of Saints Peter and Paul, after having imposed upon himself the rule of silence. He had been gathering mare's tail in a miry clearing, crouching, and with his thoughts elsewhere. The bear had emerged from the nettles, catching him unawares. It had reared up on two paws and bellowed fearsomely, spat at him, and circled him a few times. And he, forgetting his obligation, had subdued it by looking it straight in the eyes, with his right forefinger raised in the air. All in one breath he told it the charm his adoptive mother used to say to mad dogs: a string of rhyming and pagan words that he would never have believed he still remembered. The wild beast had dropped onto its forepaws and stood still, then it stretched out on its belly, with its neck and chin on the ground, and let out a fawning sound, like a whimper. When Onufrie turned his back and left, the bear submissively followed him at a distance of forty paces, without coming closer or going farther away for the length of a week, waiting for him at night in front of the cave, in the grass, and accompanying him by day on his walks to fetch wood and mushrooms, water, resin, and herbs, abandoning him only after it had been chased away with stones and grimaces, because its master wanted to await the third descent of the Virgin and Her command in solitude. There were gentler and harsher canons that he imposed upon himself throughout his time in the wilderness, as are all things in the world, from walking barefoot and endlessly repeating some prayer to carrying a heavy beechwood cross on his back and extending the black fast from new to full moon. Even his solitude had nuances, demonstrating to the grammarians that the adjective *complete* (when modifying solitude) can take degrees of comparison. It was one thing to forget the existence of his fellow men entirely and another when he encountered, albeit rarely, signs of them: the prints of a boot, a cigarette stub, an empty bottle still reeking of plum brandy, dried turds surrounded by crumpled and soiled burdock leaves. He had already notched seven lines on his finger, the last resembling a wound rather than a scar, when somewhere far off, on a peak from which he was separated by numerous precipitous valleys, men began to construct something. He could not see them, the distance was too great, nor could he make out what they were doing, but he could distinguish a mound, like a mole or a furuncle on a broad shoulder, a point that had begun to gleam both in daylight and in darkness, where they must have laid a tin roof and started up an electric generator. Later, not long after the day of May 16, on which the whetted steel scored the inside of his right forefinger, in order for blood to gush and to keep a right reckoning of the time elapsed since the appearance of the Mother of the Holy Infant, for the ninth time, from somewhere out of the fog a pylon painted red and white had

emerged, erected above that hummock, proof that it was a re-
lay for transmitters or for radio broadcasts, a cause for agitation and dejection for him, who became certain that the people
from below had gone completely mad and no longer wor-
shipped the Holy Cross but stripy poles. One night of cold
drizzle, as he was writing out rows of psalms in his spruce-
bark Bible, dipping his hawk-feather quill in the bilberry juice,
he heard a noise like thunder and went to the mouth of the
cave to watch the storm. Outside it was raining softly, but on
the far-off peak flames could be seen, as though the pylon and
the building at its base had been struck by lightning. Onufrie
blew out his candle, quickly said his prayers, and slept deeply,
with a kind of smile imprinted upon his lips and eyelids. For
the heavenly bolt of lightning had smitten the heedlessness of
the sinners. On the third morning after this occurrence, as he
was watering the wild lilac bushes, he found at the root of one
of them, the one on the eastern side, a small leather bag, tied at
the mouth with a shoelace. Inside there was a folded-up note, a
pencil, and a piece of brown, crumpled, blank paper, ready for
an answer. He did not have much to read: "I threw four grenades down the chimney. Forgive me, father!" And he stood
for a while with the note in his hand, like a moth captivated by
the flashes of the explosions, deciphering behind that careless
handwriting but correctly placed punctuation marks that his
isolation was only an illusion, that strange eyes had observed
him from the undergrowth, from crags, from the shadows of
the forest, they had learned his ways, his hours, his pleasures,
they had guessed many of the secrets of his mountain life. His
first urge had been to flee to the cave, as though there that fervent and astonishing message would have been erased and

things would have returned to the way they were before, but he ended up sitting on a jagged boulder, running his fingers through his tangled beard, looking now at the ground, now at an anthill, now at the structure that no longer smoldered, no longer glinted in the sun, and no longer supported a red-and-white-striped pole, knowing that a monk, even if he had thrown stones at a bear, was not permitted to chase away a lost sheep. About a week later, after he had come to terms with the idea that another human soul had taken shelter in that wilderness, he grasped the pencil stub and let his hand glide over the scrap of brown paper. "I, an unworthy priest, with the power that is granted to me, forgive you and absolve you from all your sins," his letter began and, before being put back into the leather pouch and hidden under the wild lilac bush, it was completed with a blessing and a lapidary explanation about how Holy Communion should be taken: a mouthful of blackberry wine, dripped into a dry acorn, stopped up with a straw. Their correspondence was to be long and intense, without ever transcending the same telegraphic style and without the correspondents ever seeing each other face to face. One sought the forgiveness of the Lord after venturing upon murky deeds, and the other, as confessor, found himself confronted with confessions he never would have imagined in the past. After the first exchange, they had switched the place in which they concealed their missives, because it seemed to the unknown person that the wild lilac bushes, arranged in a cross as they were, five along one arm and two to the right and left, might attract suspicious looks. As their mailbox, one which they used for almost six years, they chose a hole in a rock, no bigger than a fist and deep enough for the arm to reach in as far as the elbow, which they stopped up with a chalkstone. Nowadays, that man who hid his face, steps, movements, hiding places, and goals would be called an anti-Communist resistance fighter. His identity would have been lost in the ash of time and in the moldering odor of the archives of the civil list. No one would recall passages from his biography upon seeing his yellowing birth certificate or a heading in the *Registry for the Living*. Perhaps he is still alive and drawing a pension. Perhaps his bones are rotting who knows where. Back then, when they shared those hostile territories, bound to one another by rare and concise epistles, he related how, in a cabin, he had once separated the Party members from the others, made them stand to attention and sing the royal anthem, while he fried their hammer-and-sickle identity cards in oil, and then made them swallow them page by page, cover and all. He told of how he had severed the steel cable of a funicular, and how he had put a stop to a backgammon game between a sublieutenant and a warrant officer, using a bullet to perforate, from a great distance, the skull of the former, causing him to fall onto the middle of the board and scatter the chips and dice over the floor of the tavern where they were spending the afternoon. His confessions, unusual as they were, set down on paper rather than uttered beneath the stole, near the altar, were not confined to feats of arms, some unsuccessful, such as the plan to derail a military goods train that bore Cyrillic inscriptions, speeding eastward, or the attempt to save the widow who had hidden him in her orchard before she could be bundled into the back of a black Volga. They also described events without the whiff of gunpowder. For example, rolling with that widow under apple and plum trees in bloom, then laden with fruit, with mellow fruit, with fading leaves, without leaves, later budding, and once again in bloom. It is true, the unknown man did not achieve that skill of sanctimonious women in seeking blame otherwise than where they are guilty. He did not stuff the head of the priest with deviations from the strictness of fasting or the saying of prayers. He did not talk of things that others would have been eager to make known. He merely chose according to his own law what was to be confessed, once mentioning the theft of a barrel of plum brandy and, on a number of occasions, his tumblings all by himself, at moments when he was assailed by lust and delusions in the wilderness. On receiving each new letter (and months passed from one to another), Onufrie's behavior might have inspired all kinds of zoological comparisons: he rolled up and bristled like a hedgehog or retracted like a tortoise into its shell, he unfolded the notes with the fear and curiosity of a roebuck intent on the leaps and splashes of a frog, he ruminated upon the contents like a sated buffalo, and digested them long and laboriously, like a snake a mouse. He always forgave the stranger and absolved him of all his sins, even if there was a long way from the gentleness of the monk to the taking of lives, or from the flagellation of the body to its rapture. In unbroken expectation of the Mother of God, Onufrie had stumbled upon a kind of Saint George, an unseen figure, a drinker of hard liquor, hardy of limb, who fought the dragon that ruled over towns and villages, and had erected that red and white pylon in place of the Holy Cross, and cast monks, priests, and intellectuals into dungeons, the better to deceive the people. And if arms resounded and blood flowed (now and then one of the dragon's many heads was lopped off), in war it had to be thus. Both of them, ascetic and hero, did not doubt that, in such times of conflict, the air had filled with hate and thirst for vengeance (and the cloud of dust that the black Volga had raised as it vanished with the widow had looked more threatening and overwhelming than any storm cloud). As a veteran combatant inflamed by the fervor of revenge, the stranger was convinced that any action provoked repression and any ambuscade called down a blockade, not for reasons of rhyme or other strictures of poetry, but because nothing goaded an army that reckoned itself invincible more than partisans and their maddening strikes. The day was not far off when soldiers were to encircle the mountain and to search every dell, scree, wood, bush, high plateau, and slope, when (as many and as thick as the scales of the dragon, as Onufrie imagined it) they would tighten the rings of their search toward the peaks, let slip the dogs in every direction, thrust their bayonets into the molehills and rich earth of the meadows, light fires at the mouths of the caves and gullies to suffocate with smoke any living thing that might have crept there, sift every palmful of ground, in search of tracks, eager to kill and leave a stiff and cold body for the crows, eagles, and worms. And, so that at least one of them would still know the sky above his head at the end of that day, there was need for foresight and preparation, for envisaging of the greatest evil, so that an antidote might be discovered in time. To the stranger it did not seem secret enough that they used as a mailbox a hole in a rock stopped up with a chalkstone. He was afraid that, walking there too often to look for new messages, they would end up beating a track and giving themselves away. Consequently, he had invented a signaling system, by which they abided strictly over the years, so that one could find out when the other had written, and the weeds and grass could grow undisturbed around the rock, untouched by the soles of boots for months. When his deeds became too heavy and demanded to be written in an epistle to be forgiven, on a dead pine tree there would sprout a few caps of white trunk rot, fixed not too high, not too low, to be observed by eyes that understood their meaning. When they, the deeds, found absolution in the words inscribed by the servant of the Lord, the caps of trunk rot would move to a fallen plane tree. As for the missives, they were burnt soon after being read, and their ash was scattered on water, to be consumed. Their secret code was not, however, limited to announcing correspondence. Even billy goats warn the flock by a whistle when dangers arise, and she-wolves cram their cubs into holes and hollows. By concealing his appearance, name, shelters, and ways, the stranger was protecting his hide, but he could not leave his indulgent confessor to the will of chance, the confessor whom he had once espied in the company of a tame bear and had sometimes seen cutting tufts of hair from his crown and stuffing them in his pockets. Not at all preoccupied with precaution and details, just as he was not preoccupied by his ever greater resemblance to a wild beast (his beard had grown down to his bellybutton and his clothes looked like matted fur), the monk behaved like a child at peace in the days of childhood, indifferent to the enmity stirred up among men. He sought no protection, nor did he ever wish it. It somehow befell him that that man who copied something of Saint George also had the qualities of a guardian angel. And when danger appeared stones would roll from some ledge or steep gully, a beech branch would be attached to one of the spruce trees known only to them, and Onufrie, wherever he might be, would take refuge in his cave, covering the

entrance with curtains of ivy and boulders assembled before-
hand. In winter, the avalanche would be set off with snowballs,
the beech branch would be replaced with a clump of straw that
imitated a nest, and the ivy with a cut pine, thrust into the
snow. They had also agreed on a signal for terrible events, for
that unique, grave, and dizzying situation when the soldiers
would form a cordon, when the dragon would be embodied in
as many scales and begin to whistle as it searched for them. In
such circumstances, the caw of a raven would have been heard
thrice and, after a pause, twice again, then the caw would be
repeated with the same cadence, and down a high wall of ashen
rock, always dry because it faced south, water would have begun to stream and glisten in the sun. The final part of their understanding, a kind of confirmation of the dimensions and im-
minence of the danger, assumed that the stranger would be in
the vicinity of the uniformed invasion, and would be able to
demolish the sluice with which he had long ago changed the
course of a stream. However, things, as they come from God,
are not fulfillments of foresights, and so that warrior stingy in
the use of bullets and grenades (not because he had no one at
whom to aim them, but because of the precariousness of his
reserves of munitions) never had the occasion to lift the log set
in the path of the water and, even if he had done so, it would
have served no purpose, because the enemy surrounded them
one rainy morning, when the wall of the rock was wet and the
sun buried in cloud. On that unavoidable day, which Onufrie
had foreseen since the note found under the wild lilac bush and
had accepted together with the communion wine dripped little
by little into a dry acorn, on that day about which he had imagined, with shudders, so many things and which he had kept rel-

egating to the future, Onufrie was molding candles from wasp's wax, carefully inserting the wick into the yellowish paste. First, he wondered at the bird that was groping around in the loud and tireless downpour outside, then he dropped the boiling vessel, without feeling the scald on the back of his hands, and went out into the rain dragging behind him the bunches of ivy from above the entrance, without stopping to pile the boulders one on top of another. He fled to the brook on the left of the cave (as he had been instructed in one of the letters) and, treading along the narrow streambed, he climbed until he found the hazel tree that leaned over the stream. He caught hold of its stem and climbed without touching the earth so as not to leave tracks for the men and dogs. He crossed into the next tree, holding onto the slippery branches, and thence into the pine tree in which he had prepared his hiding place. He did not tremble, he did not lose his poise, nor did he bother to listen to the voices that at one point passed beneath him. In his nostrils he caught the scent of cigarette smoke, and he glimpsed military berets. He kept trying to determine whether the eyes of the Immaculate Virgin also had the color of military kit.

For a long time, from the autumn of the dragon's fury until the autumn that followed and another three seasons, he received no more tidings from the stranger. Sometimes he thought him dead, sometimes alive. He prayed for him, knowing that prayer slips in where thought does not succeed. He had sometimes been ready to revive the powers of holy unction, but he had refrained from performing such a mass so as not to oblige good to bring forth evil and, God forbid, for evil to triumph from their separation. During the whole of the hiatus in their correspondence and his return to unbroken hermit solitude in the wilderness, he added countless passages to his strange Gospel, which meant not only large steps forward along the paths of the Savior and of the Virgin (above all the Virgin!), but also an alarming, unimaginable growth in the proportions of the work. As well as being an approximate reconstruction of the words and the miracles of the Mother and of the Son, that Bible proved in practical terms to be a huge body, made up of thousands or tens of thousands of long strips of wood, as wide as or a little wider than laths, a corpus that expanded from one week to the next through the addition of new verses and, implicitly, new bundles of spruce bark. There was barely room in the cave for a bed or a corner in which to sit. The icon screen, painted with dyes squeezed from all kinds of plants, had also been obscured by the voluminous sheaves, and Onufrie found himself forced to write, cook, eat, craft, and pray in a space as cramped as a closet. As for the possibility of re-reading older fragments of his Scripture, even if there had been a passage between the stacks of bark (arranged in distinct books and chapters), the text stretched the full length of the cave, so that the beginning and the sections that followed it—early episodes, the Nativity, scenes from the childhood of Christ or, in other words, from the tender and unblemished youth of Mary—had remained at the back, crowded together. And it had become very hard to break through that far because of the labyrinthine paths, the spider webs, rockslides, and darkness; the candles would go out on the way due to the lack of air and even if they had burned properly, it still would have been of no help, because the wood had moldered or shriveled, and might have caught fire at any time. Then, supposing that he had found the paragraph he was looking for—and there was a good chance, because he had not worked at random, but in order and with scrupulousness—what could he have deciphered on tree bark used as paper when it was white and smooth, still full of sap, but which had now cracked and crumbled to pieces? However, what had been finished long ago counted less. The hawk feathers were always sharp and dipped in bilberry juice. Such nibs and such ink brought forth new words, one line called upon another, and time slipped by with its precarious units of measure: the cropping of the tuft of bluish-black hair, the seasons, day and night, the years numbered since the appearance of the Immaculate Virgin near a copper mine. He had notched the seventeenth line on his right forefinger and the knife-cut was caught beneath a thick blackish scab, when one warm morning, the caps of white trunk rot appeared once more on the dead pine. They had recently been broken off, and were white underneath and light gray above. He had almost forgotten the path to the mailbox, in front of which had sprouted a wild rosebush. Rummaging in the hole in the rock, the thorns scratched his arms. The leather pouch, faded and patched on one side, was tied at the mouth as ever. The note inside informed him that the men in uniform had declared an amnesty and explained that alluring word differently from all the dictionaries, which attempt to propagate the idea that freedom can be granted, and not just won. With his fingertips he touched the page, torn from an exercise book: on one side there were a child's calculations, addition and subtraction, on the other, the text no longer resembled a telegram, but still scorned calligraphic elegance. The stranger did not urge him to return to his fellows, though he believed that sooner or later Onufrie would decide to descend into the world. And he advised the monk to dress like all the others, to cut his beard and his hair short, to be reticent and taciturn as a shadow lost among the bodies of the living ("it is the time of shadows," argued the stranger, "shadows slip through their fingers!"). He advised him to avoid sparsely populated places, monasteries, villages, building sites, farms, where curious eyes and sly tongues would all too soon find out too much about him, enough to whisper it elsewhere and to write informative notes to the secret police. He begged him to go to the big cities, because he would be safer in the crowds than among a few souls. Onufrie was in no hurry to abandon the mountains. He kept writing and writing, at first, briefly and affectionately, an epistle in which he blessed the stranger and absolved him from his sins for the last time, and then his own Gospel, the one he could not compress and did not want to abandon. To make room for the sheaves of wood that contained the acts of the Virgin before Her Ascension, he moved his belongings outside and slept for a few weeks under a canopy of fir needles, a kind of tent. He wrote in all weather, and sacrificed dozens of pieces of bark, arranging them over his head like tiles so that the raindrops would not mingle with the bilberry juice and turn the letters into violet stains. One gloomy, misty sunset, he lit the fire to warm himself and boil water for herbal tea, and then wrote until midday, after which, without cleaning the hawk feathers as he did after every other pause, he had walled up the mouth of the cave. He laid the boulders in rows, putting similar shapes and sizes alongside each other, with edges of a suitable fit. He used yellow, sticky earth mixed with sand as mortar. While there was still some time until sunset, he sharpened the scissors he had received from Father Nae and, along with his bluish-black tuft, he had cut his hair and trimmed his beard. He laid rows of ivy over the newly constructed wall and set off downhill in the dark, with two baskets full of blackberries, one to exchange for old clothes, the other to pay a barber to shave him with a razor. He did not murmur prayers or psalms, but instead sang a ditty about a tomcat as big as a kitten. Behind him remained a host of peeled spruce trees in the forest.

⤙⤚

From practicing so many trades he did not become inured to any single one; he had a multitude of occupations, each for a week or two at a time, never more than eleven weeks. He had been in turn a stoker, porter, bricklayer, sweeper, upholsterer, drayman, jeweler, stacker, circus hand, stretcher-bearer, truck loader, gravedigger, baker, and plenty of other things, always wearing the canvas hat he had obtained in return for a basket of wild blackberries, and which was wonderfully suited to the times. The facts, however, were simpler than all those job titles, and the resemblances between the trades clearer than the distinctions, because to be a stoker, bricklayer, stacker, drayman, or baker had meant for him, since his time as a novice, just one thing—to lift from dawn to dusk, usually carrying the loads on his back, sometimes in his arms. Only the load differed, first coal and beech wood, then cement and mortar, crates of nails and screws, planks and beams, sacks of flour and yeast. Then he had lumped into the same category, that of cleaning, the jobs of sweeper, upholsterer, jeweler, and circus hand, collecting the dust, trash, and leaves from the boulevards, washing all kinds of plush and woolen stuffing, hosing down the bodywork of the trucks and trailers in a garage, polishing brass until it looked like gold and nickel until it passed for silver, mucking out the cages of wild beasts, especially the box of a bear weakened by dysentery, a creature he thought he had seen before. Among all those occupations, the job of stretcher-bearer had proven to be a combination of many others, a mixture of porter (except with a white smock) and cleaning woman (except he was a man). He bore people who had suffered heart attacks, fractures, strokes, peritonitis, poisoning, ulcers or perforated intestines, fainting, pneumonia, burns, pancreatitis, renal blockages, and countless other misfortunes of the flesh. He took them by stretcher from the ambulances to the emergency rooms, from the emergency rooms to the wards, from the wards to the laboratories or operating theaters, thence back to the wards and, sadly, sometimes to the small morgue in the grounds. On the other hand, he was also made to scrub the floors of the hospital corridors and waiting rooms (and how much there was to scrub! And behind his wet cloths boots and shoes would once more tread, and it would all have to be scrubbed again). As a gravedigger, he attended a single burial, after the bear with dysentery died and a few other circus hands had wrapped it in plastic sheeting to give to the dustmen in the morning. He had heard about it from a former workmate he had bumped into on the tram. He went to the menagerie that night and stole the corpse. He dug the grave in a park, far from the streetlights, in pitch darkness, listening for every sound, especially the footsteps of the militiamen who patrolled the lanes with a lantern. Finally, he had taken off his canvas cap, cut the tuft on his forehead, and cast it into the grave, on top of the bear. He had whispered the burial service by the light of a candle. He had wept. Then he had picked up his shovel and covered that body that ought to have rotted in the mountains, not in the middle of the largest city. Only as a watchman had he managed to rest. In fact, the day after the burial, he had rested too long, until they found him fast asleep in the hall of the building where he was supposed to be on watch, at around lunchtime, curled up by the radiator. During all of this urban period, a little over two years, he did not go hungry except of his own will, when he fasted, and he slept under the open sky only when he wanted to drink in the spring air or to close his eyes beneath the hosts of stars. He had food on the table and a roof over his head. He changed job after job and place after place not because he was inconstant—that was just the way it happened. Everywhere he was taciturn and submissive until someone took the Lord's name in vain, until he felt he was being pumped for information or followed, until he witnessed dirty tricks like those of the jeweler, or the builders, who pilfered from the sacks, from the bricks he carried, until he was cornered by a woman (in the upholstery workshop, a freckled woman had felt his bottom and between his legs and kept trying to put her breast in his face), until he was struck (the driver, a tawny-haired ox, had punched him for not having emptied out the ashtray in the cab of his truck), until he caught someone rummaging through his things (as in the bakery), or until his illusions and fervor came to naught (in the hospital, where he had stayed longer than anywhere else, eleven weeks, imagining that he was helping the sick and worried relatives, he woke up one day next to two individuals on a stretcher, a father and mother of children, both married, an engineer and a draftswoman, caught coiled together on a desk, like two mounting dogs, in other words the classic medical condition known as *penis captivus*).

Then he thought that, given the way history was heading, the
Holy Virgin should have been disgusted at cities and averted
Her eyes from them, but he was sure that She would not allow
Herself to be overcome by anger and would seek to spread joy,
at least crumbs of joy, where there was so much sadness and
where so much vileness was perpetrated. He awaited Her fe-
verishly (on streets, in squares, in shops, in buses), fearful lest
Her sign come unexpectedly and pass unheeded. He knew that
the Immaculate Virgin might be incarnated anywhere and any
time, without being confused by the fact that he had rewritten
his biography and identity in order to live among men. As for
men, even if few of them wore uniforms, they all behaved as
though the buttons, epaulettes, and belts had entered their in-
nards, they had become accustomed to breathing barracks air,
out of fear, self-interest, resignation, and indolence. Dwell-
ing in big cities, lost in the crowd, he nevertheless also saw the
good side of things: he had given up being his own confessor,
because it would have been a sin to continue to do so when he
could be shriven by a priest; every four hours he found a dust-
bin in which to throw away his bluish-black tuft; every day he
entered a church (always a different one, so as not to attract attention) and prayed before the icons of the Mother of God; he
was no longer forced to crochet and tailor garments from his
own hair, as he received plenty of clothes as funeral alms; he
was never absent from the holy liturgy on Sundays and feast
days; sometimes he would be warm when outside the frost was
splitting the paving stones; he cracked red Easter eggs and answered "Truly He is risen!" to "Christ is risen!" Above all,
a Bible once more came into his hands, one different in form
and dimension from that confused Bible he had walled into his

cave: one with a dog-eared brown cover and stained, yellow-ing pages. He read and he read, he read until he grew weary of hiding in the crowd and boarded the first train leaving from the largest station of the largest city.

Rumors and tales were born in those years, too. It was eas-ier to speak of miracles than of collectivized land. Miracles passed as the delusions of old biddies, whereas discussions re-garding the shooting of horses, or about wool, grain, and egg quotas led to interrogations and reprisals. Onufrie roamed through villages and towns, attentive to the chatter at the gates, to the whispers in churches and graveyards. He was seeking tidings of possible deeds of the Virgin, following not the epic thread of the narratives but their geographic settings, hoping to discover them throughout a wide expanse of the earth and examine each one closely. He set out toward the tears of chrism shed by the Mother of God in a village in Vlashca (as it was known in the days before the Communists). There, in front of a cordon of soldiers who were surrounding the church, he found a motley and weary crowd—the infirm of every variety (blind, mute, paralytic, deaf, epileptic) accompanied by moth-ers, fathers, husbands, brothers, bands of Gypsies, infants, women weeping for all so many reasons (some caressing pho-tographs), seminarians, secret policemen, dozing old folk, all kinds of gawpers, monks and nuns, tractor drivers, and shep-herds. The parish priest had not been seen for four days, since the day he had given statements to the militia in a building more attractive than the rest in town, with dusty photographs of suspected poultry thieves in its windows. A petty trade had sprung up as the crowd waited for the priest; a wizened Gypsy woman and another with a nose like a potato were selling toasted sunflower seeds, and a sprightly young lass had ventured out with gingerbread and a demijohn of elderflower cordial. Earlier, an old man had tried his luck at selling crucifixes carved from linden wood, but he had been driven away by the lieutenant in the blue uniform. During the week he spent alongside the others under the open sky, Onufrie did not hear the bells toll. The verger had been ordered not to leave his house, and a soldier, changed every six hours, guarded the entrance. Onufrie gazed at the crows resting on the cross at the tip of the spire, the clouds of dust over the plain, and the gleam of sunset on the river. He heard some people saying that tears had flowed from the right eye of the Immaculate Virgin and stopped at Her chin, others that they had streamed from both eyes, reached the cheekbones, and dripped onto the floor. He ate mulberries, a lump of cold maize porridge given to him by a small girl, two buns acquired from a widow. One morning he had to lie and say that he had an upset stomach, then get up from the grass and vanish for a while, when a man sat down next to him dressed in clothes that were too clean and too folksy, who kept blathering about human stupidity and the fraud the priest had committed by dripping oil onto a wretched icon with a pipette. The man had singled the monk out, and on Onufrie's return, even though he had been gone for over an hour, gave him a friendly slap on the back and went on stringing together his vile remarks, about the money, rugs, dishes, and towels brought by the faithful and carted off home by the priest's wife, about the priest's definite connections to the bandits in the mountains, about the inclinations of the priest's son, a lad of nine, toward fascist literature, about what good fortune it was that the Interior Ministry's troops had arrived to save the village from such swindles. At this point, Onufrie struck the man, kicking him hard in the testicles. Then he fled over the stubble fields and between the rows of maize, toward a wood. He was convinced that the Holy Mother of God would impart Her plan to him at another time, a day later, eighty days later, maybe a thousand days later. He set off down a cart track, came to a railway line and followed it to the left, then he melted into the distance. He reappeared later (three years must have passed) as a follower of Sandica, the Trumpet of God, an ema- ciated girl with one eye missing, the other hazel, who was trun- dled around in a cart covered by an awning. She was always stretched out, wrapped either in thick blankets or only a sheet, the veins on her temples and on the backs of her hands ap- peared now bluish, now gray (depending on the light of the sun and her mood), she drank only water and ate only boiled fish (which her attendants cleaned of bones, mashed into a paste, and fed her with a spoon), she slept a lot, exhausted by her gift (at each occurrence she would be bathed in streams of sweat and the women washed her in her sleep, taking care not to wake her, anointed her with oils to preserve her scent of roses, and changed the sheets), she laughed rarely (once a sea- son), sometimes she asked for wild flowers (especially bunches of daisies), whenever she screamed long and piercingly they would stop the cart or abandon what they were doing and crowd around her, on their knees, with their brows to the ground, their hands clasped at their breasts, letting her writhe with her black hair untrammeled, drinking in her words one by one and all at once, except that they were not her words — only the lips and the tongue were hers — but the words of the Sav- ior, uttered for all mortals, but heard first by them, the attendants of His Trumpet. And they in their turn ate only boiled fish and quenched their thirst only with water. They did not even permit themselves to drink tea. They always went on foot, in front of and behind the cart with the awning. Their endless wandering had no destinations. Their goal appeared to be to roam, to disseminate that long and piercing scream and the words of Christ, in as many places as possible, not necessarily that it might reach the ears of men but that it might be borne on the wind like pollen and settle like hoarfrost. They were not many, sometimes six or seven, at other times up to thirty. At one point they had agreed to get rid of Sandica's aura of virginity, on finding out that the blue uniforms wanted to scatter them and intern her in a hospice. They had gone to the registry office of a small town, from which they departed with a certificate of marriage between the Trumpet of God and Jancu, a skillful fisherman of chub and barbel in rivers, trout in mountain lakes, and perch, carp, and dace in the Delta, a young man who had known her since she was little, since her parents began to keep her in the henhouse and to feed her along with the fowls. Under the cover of that official document on which were blazoned the arms and the name of the republic, her virginity remained intact and her fame faded away. It was around this time that Onufrie joined them, when the inhabitants of the settlements through which they passed no longer paid them any heed, or even jeered them, after the blue uniforms let it be known that Sandica had married (and whoever had heard of a wife that remained a virgin? Whoever had heard of a saint who willingly gave up her virginity?). This was the time when an American landed on the moon, and many a villain, some who concealed epaulettes and military stripes beneath their garb, others who did not even bother, spread the news that, ever since Sandica had found out what a tool was, her husband was not enough for her and she summoned all the men under her awning in turn, and made them satisfy all her pleasures; why else would she scream so long and piercingly? In such circumstances, Sandica's attendants looked with enmity upon the man with the canvas cap who had waited for them at a crossroads. They tried to drive him away a few times (with stones, with threatening fists), they had kept him at a distance for a while, they did not accept him until the day on which they thought they had got rid of him. But he had returned toward evening and placed at their feet a fish longer than a goose and fatter than a turkey, with scales like golden coins, with a tail two palms wide, a fish such as they had never seen and which must have weighed more than thirty pounds. Their mistrust soon returned when one of them noticed that the man's short disappearances occurred with an almost clockwork precision every four hours. They feared he was sending signals to the blue uniforms who would then discover their ever more roundabout and convoluted routes, but in just what manner he might be doing so they could not imagine, since the newcomer neither lit fires, nor released homing pigeons, nor had a rucksack or other luggage that might conceal a transmitter; he did not cry out, nor did he imitate the sounds of animals. One morning Jancu sneaked after him into a thicket of elderberries and white poplar, and brought them the answer: the gloomy man with the scar-notched finger, about whom he (Jancu) had said from the very start that there was something unclean (no one could have caught such a carp with hook and line), had cut from his crown a thick bunch of hair and left it among the leaves, so that the soldiers' dogs might pick up their trail. They accused, Onufrie felt no need to exonerate himself, and merely asked them to be patient until evening. And, as he never had since his childhood, he went bareheaded, so that all could be witness and understand. They stood around him, they did not leave him for a single moment, they watched in amazement as the tuft grew before their very eyes, straight upward, bristly and tar black, different from the slicked-back hair riddled with white strands, they watched as it lengthened and swelled like a large pinecone, as it began to discolor, to soften and ooze a purplish ichor before he lopped it off with the scissors. Until sunset came (it was a Wednesday, and the sun had sunk hazily, foretelling a rainy Thursday), they were witness to the cycle another three times, piteous, remorseful, as dumb as boiled fish. And on Thursday, it did indeed rain and when they awoke they found him at the mouth of the awning, speaking with Sandica in a whisper. She was turning in her lap a large bouquet of daisies, which he must have picked in the night. Afterward he left, with the canvas cap on his head, through a field of barley, northeastward. He passed through the portal of Neamtz Monastery on Saturday at around lunchtime and by vespers he was already wearing a habit and kamelavkion. In the first month after his return he took care to weave a blackish carpet, as stiff as if it had been made of horsehair, which he laid before the old icon of the Mother of God.

For more than twenty years he knelt on that harsh carpet, always examining the small scratch on the thigh of the Holy Child, praying, wearying himself in one way, but maintaining his fervor and patience in another, slowly turning white, growing thinner, frailer, discovering new interpretations for what had been and unimagined paths to what was to be, accustoming himself to his ever more leathery and wrinkled skin and to dizzy spells, sometimes suffocating when the light of the sun and the candles would go black as he rose to his feet. Once he even collapsed there, before the icon of the Holy Mother, when the church was empty and a tiny spider had just caught a fly in its web above the pulpit. They found him stretched out on the cold flagstones, though he was still warm, his knees on the carpet. The monks had tripped over their own vestments, and each other, in fear and confusion. The nurse and the ambulance driver had crossed themselves on arrival and, when leaving, with the tips of their tongues against the roofs of their mouths because their hands were full. The stretcher-bearers had taken away the inert body, laughing at the bluish-black tuft when his kamelavkion had fallen off and rolled over the floor, and the physicians had diagnosed a stroke. The whole of his left side was paralyzed and he could barely move his right hand; what the mirror in the ward showed when it met his face was hideous and painful. At first they spoon-fed him through the corner of his mouth, they put a bedpan in his bed, and an asthmatic young man from the country—having managed to decipher a note Onufrie wrote in three quarters of an hour, consisting of a single sentence—used to cut the tuft of hair on his crown six times a day. Then things abated: the soup no longer ran down his beard, and the noodles no longer hung from his lips, he ventured to utter words without taking fright on hearing them, he had thrust the Bible toward the young man with the effort he formerly would have exerted to shift a sack of coal or a barrel of pickled cabbage, and he once more used the scissors from Father Nae, although it was not he who sharpened them, nor did he handle them. He arrived at the baths of that town in the mountains the following summer, when he could already speak, though with a slur and too many *h*'s, but clearly enough for the employees of the spa to understand and answer him. He could chew his food, wrap himself up in bed, and arrange his pillow unaided, he could go to the window using a banister fixed to the wall, dragging his left leg behind the right. He would look out at the woods, the sunlit crests, and patches of sky, sometimes through the dirty windowpanes he was only able to distinguish wet trees, mist, and clouds (and how swiftly raced the clouds!), he would be taken to the treatment rooms in a wheelchair, he read, he hankered for sweets and gave a nurse money to buy him candy and Turkish delight, he prayed in the dark, although not for the healing of his body split in two like many others in this world, but for the salvation of the soul that remained in the healthy half, though his heart was in the sick half. He would sometimes watch television—whether he liked it or not, because the will of the majority was decisive at the sanatorium too—after massages, hot towels, ionized baths, physiotherapy and electrotherapy, after midday meals and sleep.

About that evening, all his roommates had something to tell, to comment on, to add, even though one of them should have serenely held his tongue, because he had been in the yard, playing whist, and the other three, who had been watching an entire documentary about the breast-feeding of baby whales, would not admit, even under torture, that it had not seemed anything unusual to them at the time. Rheumatic No. 1, for example, upheld that he felt a draught of hot air that had made his blanket flutter and forced him to take off his braided vest midway through the film; the fat man with kidney stones claimed that the monk had swallowed some large red pills on the sly, while pretending to watch the broadcast; the mining engineer struck down with silicosis said that he had caught the old man walking and swinging his arms without difficulty, but had kept it a secret to see just how far the imposture would stretch; rheumatic No. 2, the one who had gone outside to smoke and kill some time playing cards, swore that the old man had become phosphorescent a week before the whole business and that he, as an insomniac, had studied at length the greenish rays he emitted — in fact he had even been able to solve a crossword in the dark by their light. Onufrie's own version of his miraculous recovery of health (he had gotten out of bed at the end of that documentary, he had run toward the television set with hands raised and fingers spread, he had fallen to his knees sobbing loudly, moaning, choking, groaning, he had stammered unintelligible things and rubbed his forehead against the carpet until he flayed the skin) was that *for a third time the Mother of God had descended to show him Her succor and faith.* She had leaned Her delicate shoulder against the television set, touched by the tenderness of the mother whales and by the awkwardness of the baby whales, She had commanded him to rise up and walk (as the Son also had done with the daughter of Jairus and with the paralytic) and She had entrusted him, when he no longer even dreamed that it would be possible, with Her task. This, at least, is what he told his disciples and assistants with whom he was building the monastery at Red Rock, in the place and in the manner decided by Her.

⇥⇤

CHAPTER SEVEN

T HE WAY THE CARPENTER'S mate had described it, a torrent of human bones had not tumbled from the sky, like rain,
but emerged from the earth. Onufrie, who had left the clearing
at Red Rock with surplice and stole tucked under his arm, with
swift steps, with pieces of frankincense in his pockets and eight
candles in his hand, could see the torrent from above. From the
treeless corner of the path the fort looked like an ants' nest. He
felt a warm breath of wind (even if the wind was not blowing) as soon as he caught sight of that far-off crowd. In the
haste of his descent, the censer kept knocking against trees
and his belt buckle, sounding now muffled, now like sleigh
bells, mostly drowning out his murmuring (prayers or grum-
bles) and dampening the zeal of the disciple, who, as quiet as a
mouse, kept twirling his sideburns. At the edge of the wood a
soldier jumped out in front of them, begging them not to tell
anyone, especially not the officers, that they had found him
sleeping. His tunic was rumpled, covered in blades of grass and
pine needles, and the buttons were undone. It is likely that he
had been dreaming sweetly, because his eyes were still milky.
He was called Butylkin or something of the sort, his first name
was definitely Andrei. He showed them the shortest way to the
fort and told a tangled tale about skulls, lots of skulls, he used

quite a few words in Russian, which they did not understand. Farther downhill, on the slope above the fortifications, Onufrie stopped twice and made the sign of the cross: first of all when he came across a dromedary (its forelegs tethered, munching blackberry and dandelion shoots, well curried and indifferent to the swarms of flies, a great big camel such as the Virgin, Joseph, and the Holy Child must have met aplenty during their flight to Egypt), then when the pit suddenly appeared to them from between the ruins, close by, not three hundred feet away, wider than it was deep, ruddy because of the clayey earth and the afternoon sun, with white spots here and there, surrounded by a crowd of people, most of them in uniform. At his second pause, he raised his right forefinger and uttered that phrase which, according to him, summed up and comprehended all, a simple enunciation about the descents of the Mother of God. The exact words could not be heard in the valley, as there was a din around the mass grave, and in any case sounds rise rather than fall. But even if they had broken through that far and had been heard clearly, it is hard to guess what those men in uniform would truly have understood, although the words directly concerned them, because it was they who had struck him in the courtyard of the monastery, who had bundled him into a truck with a tarpaulin and sentenced him to forced labor, who had hunted him for seventeen years after his escape and had not managed to capture him, who had later played all kinds of dirty tricks on him, and who now, in just a few minutes, were to be present as he conducted a service and scattered incense smoke over the bones and over their uncovered heads, whether bowed or not. It was also then, at their second pause, that the carpenter's mate noticed how the priest's beard had bristled slightly.

At the edge of that huge grave, without any cross (when so many crosses would have been fitting), Onufrie began the burial service, convinced that no one else had done so at the proper time and that the dead had gone to the other world unshriven and without candles. He continued with all the offices for the dead and with a service of absolution for the bones and he ended with the Akathistos Hymn of the Forty Martyrs of Sevasta, in a shorter form than he used in church, because the candles had already burned down to the size of thimbles and he had become exceedingly hoarse. During the ceremony, most of the crowd had lost patience, they shuffled from one foot to another, clasped their hands behind them, in front of them, felt around in their pockets with their fingertips, coughed, yawned, sneezed, fidgeted, sought and sometimes found ways to relieve the boredom, whispering among themselves or busying themselves with little things. The priest had involuntarily noticed a young officer who was reading a folded-up newspaper, another, bald officer in a navy blue uniform who was cutting his nails and cuticles with a pair of clippers, a plump little woman who was jotting something down in a notebook, a somnolent chubby man in a beige suit, and a man in a checked shirt who, from time to time, was taking cautious nibbles from a slice of toast. Conducting the service at the western side of the mass grave, moved by the fate of the living who had become so many dead and worried at the fate of the dead from whom had resulted a thousand-fold more bones, he had heard a number of times the roars of the gelded and haughty dromedary from the slope toward the wood and had met, among dozens of faces, a gaze that chilled. The dromedary was roaring at the hymns of eternal remembrance and did not cease until a little man with a camera around his neck gave a whistle. The face of the oldest among the officers was withered, with sharp cheekbones. In the crowd there was also a pair of flashing eyes, belonging to another old man, one with teeth too white not to be false, eyes that kept blinking and were watering, probably because of the sun that shone straight into them as it sank westward. In the end, when Onufrie and the boy with sawdust in his eyebrows were preparing to return to the clearing at Red Rock, the little man had asked forgiveness for the enthusiasm of the dromedary, the old man in the linen suit had kissed his hand before Onufrie managed to withdraw it, a policeman with a mustache had thanked him in his own way, with dissembling and halting words that smelled of onions, and one of the officers, the one in a navy blue uniform, had arrived as a mere courier with a question from the commandant: why and how far was he sure that those people, the dead, were Christians and had need of such a service? As he was climbing the slope to the monastery, the plump little woman had caught up with him, holding a small device like a radio, which, however, did not play or speak but slowly hummed when she pressed a button and held it to the priest's mouth.

By dawn the next day, before he woke his oversleeping disciples, Onufrie had become, without his knowledge or desire, the hero of a newspaper article titled "A Monk Blesses the Bones of the Martyrs."

➤>◄←

CHAPTER EIGHT

THE STORY OF THAT journey foretold in the coffee grounds
did not come to an end when it appeared to have come to an end
(perhaps because of the slightly squashed heart and the peevish
little dog). Auntie Paulina returned from Mount Olympus at
around lunchtime, in the middle of a downpour. She alighted
from the bus tanned and flushed from the journey, without an
umbrella, in a calico dress printed with fishes. The rain left no
time for embraces, and we did not kiss each other on the cheek
until we reached the awning of a newspaper stand, where I also
gave her my bunch of roses. I draped my coat over her shoulders, saw to the luggage, and went off in search of a taxi. It was
pelting down with rain, and the line of taxis at the entrance to
the park had vanished, as if they had taken cover somewhere
dry. It took a quarter of an hour before a white Skoda showed
up (looking like a motorboat, said a shivering Auntie, the image
of little island ports still fresh in her mind). She sat on the back
seat. I sat next to the driver, a burly, surly type, who was speaking ill of meteorologists. At home, I rubbed myself down, put
on some warm, dry clothes, drank a cup of tea, drank a glass
of cherry liqueur, and decided that a fire in the stove would not
be a bad idea in such weather. But Auntie did not recover, even
after a hot bath, nor after tea and aspirins, nor after sitting with

her feet in a basin of steaming water and salt crystals. She was trying to smile, to be nice ("Have a little patience for the presents, darling," she told me; then she promised that she would tell me all about it, about everything under the moon and stars after she had warmed up a little; later, purplish-white, as if the towel had wiped off her tan, sneezing all the time, her eyes watery, she asked to be left alone, to compose herself, and to rest after the seventeen-hour journey; she also asked me to look after the roses). I laid the table with plates and glasses from the vitrine, with starched napkins and cutlery from a drawer of the sideboard, with tapering candles in the candlesticks I had found in a cupboard—Jojo had rubbed them with vinegar to bring them back to life. I warmed up the joint of veal prepared according to the recipe of the pigeon hunter, but Auntie did not wake up for a late lunch, nor for dinner. The storm outside had long since headed south and the sun had come out, and then the sun left too, heading west, and the moon arrived, half a moon in fact. When it grew dark and the stars came out, I listened carefully at her door, and what was audible from the room did not sound good. I entered cautiously. Paulina was shivering under her woolen bedspread, she was tossing from side to side, groaning faintly, moaning, muttering all kinds of things, wheezing. She was bathed in sweat, drenched, as though she had been rained on in her bed. I set the vase of roses on the nightstand. It was no help. Her brow was burning. I called for an ambulance. It arrived shortly before midnight, with a young medical assistant and a stretcher-bearer who took upon himself the role of a physician. Auntie was sleeping, actually, she was not sleeping, nor was she awake. She was burning, and so we wrapped her up in blankets, lifted her onto the stretcher, and set off to the hospital. The siren of the ambulance had not been switched on, and that reassured me; it allowed me to hope that this was nothing serious. However, the emergency room doctor, woken from slumber, began to bustle around her, having apparently lent an ear to the opinions of the stretcher-bearer, and sent me out of the examination room. He needed coffee and was swiftly given it: a nurse passed along the corridor with the steaming pot and the aroma made me think of morning. It was cold. The neon light on the ceiling resembled no other neon light: it did not flicker, it did not drone, instead it chilled the air. I patrolled in front of the closed door, I read all the notices on the walls, including a text about influenza vaccine, a kind of pharmaceutical poem in which *flu* rhymed with *ague, prevention* with *attention, vaccine* with *clean, fever* with *reliever,* etc., a text accompanied by two depictions of the Giaconda, one with her classic facial expression, a flacon of the medicine hanging from her neck, the other a febrile, obviously unvaccinated Mona Lisa, with all the signs of illness on her face. I coughed significantly a few times, and with the toe of my shoe I adjusted all the chair legs until they were in military alignment: they must have heard me from within, but they were too busy to care about me. Some time later, I ran out of patience. I had to know what was happening. I tapped on the door of the room. No one answered. And the door was locked. I knocked again and in my mind a film sequence began to unreel, in which the doctor had his trousers around his ankles and the plump nurse was lying on a desk among registers, prescriptions, stamps, paperclips, and pencils, on top of a stethoscope that happened to be right under her bottom. He had lifted the skirts of his medical coat and covered her mouth with his hand so that the panting sounds would not disturb Auntie's sleep. The nurse was holding her knees crooked and rapidly moving her plump hips, the doctor too was moving, more jerkily, and at this point the dumpy nurse finally opened the door, with her uniform in order, unruffled. Film and reality slightly resembled each other, however: the nurse did indeed have her mouth covered, but with her own forefinger, a sign for me not to speak too loudly, and also there was Paulina asleep, the sleeve of her sweater rolled up for the drip. Poor Auntie! After she had stood for so long in the rain, now they had placed bags of ice on her forehead and under her arms. They told me that it was a lung inflammation, that they had to get her fever down at all costs, that they had resorted to powerful antibiotics, and that she was not conscious. Then the nurse told me to leave the room, she gave me a gentle shove from behind, and in the corridor she whispered that if the doctor got angry he would wake up the whole hospital with his shouting. However irascible he may have been, the doctor was now dozing in an armchair, with one eye on the drip and the other on the patient's jerks and starts. Outside again, I too dozed off, I even fell asleep on the chairs I had lined up earlier, and before the sun arrived, heading eastward, I was given a cup of coffee by the plump nurse, who, I expect, had found the money I had slipped into her pocket. I learned that Auntie Paulina's temperature had gone down, it had fallen to thirty-eight point seven, that she had woken up at one point and was frightened by the unknown place, that she had walked on her own legs (supported, it is true) to the toilet, and that they had moved her during the latter part of the night from the emergency room into a ward with three beds, for the moment empty. I found her without the drip, still sleeping, with a film of dried sweat on her brow, which was burning, but not as fiercely as before. In the corridor, I met the doctor, who was yawning loudly and smoking by an open window. "A nasty business," he told me, "but it will turn out fine." He explained pneumonia to me and the treatment to follow, stubbed out his cigarette on the window ledge, and asked what kind of folk the Argentineans were who had recently appeared at the mass grave.

⤙⤚

As soon as they arrived in the town, the Argentinean anthropologists had confounded a number of expectations. They turned up without warning in a minibus one Wednesday morning, disappointing all those who had been imagining a festive reception at the train station, organized in advance, with the blue-and-white-striped football shirts of Batistuta and Maradona, with a brass band, with the mayor wearing a tricolor sash and giving a speech of welcome, with the new French teacher translating into Spanish and herself reminiscent of the Andean olive complexion with her bronzed calves and knees, with little girls presenting flowers, with mutton sausages and beer dispensed to the onlookers by the local branch of the party in government. Four of the Argentineans were wearing jeans and a fifth Bermuda shorts, the T-shirt of one had sleeves shredded with a pair of scissors, the vest of another was imprinted with the face of the Pope, at the throat of the tallest swung a crucifix as big as a communion-wafer stamp. In short, they looked different from the way men of science usually appear in the popular imagination and were younger than they ought to have been. Moreover, to speak of them as men of science is not entirely correct. For the group numbered three men and two women, which thus diminished by almost half the dreams of conquering hearts and crossing the ocean that some young misses had been nurturing.

At the mass grave site, where there were so many controversies, passions, and suspicions about the time and circumstances of the deaths, the five had been regarded as saviors. Only Providence could have sent them from the shores of the Rio de la Plata estuary to the other end of the world, to a castrum abandoned by Aurelian to the barbarians and the passing centuries, to study heaps of bones, while being objective regarding the recent history of the place in which they had landed, and to give a clarifying verdict, with loaded local and national consequences. In anticipation of the airplane that had set off over two confluent rivers, the Paraná and the Uruguay, a single general satisfaction had taken shape in that mountain town: the story of the mass grave was nearing an end. The aircraft that would fly over the town, the mountains, and the Roman fortifications had given birth to lots of hopes, some of them openly confessed, most of them secret. The chief of police, for instance, who kept monotonously and more and more unconvincingly preaching his theory of a summary execution in the '50s, would have given up much in the world, even onions, to hear the passengers of the plane attesting to a political crime. He was not as worried about the interviews and declarations with which he had busied himself since early summer coming back to haunt him, as he was about a rumor that was no longer a rumor but factual information regarding his premature transferral to the reserve. As seekers of sensationalism and crafters of reputations, having supported the version and idiosyncrasies of the major, having described him as a lawman who was exposing a dreadful murder and a cover-up, most of the journalists were also counting on a showy conclusion by the strangers from the other hemisphere. They too wanted a confirmation of all they had put on paper or uttered into microphones for weeks on end. Titus Maeriu—having spent years of his life behind bars, having endured torture, and knowing that tens of thousands of others had been unable to endure the unendurable and had passed to the next world, amazed that his supposed freedom after amnesty had been limited to marriage and a doctoral thesis on tunnel resistance in strata of sedimentary rock, convinced that those who had left the prisons for heaven had grown wings and were seated on the right hand of the Father, aware that he did not deserve more than them, wondering whether or not he had been the more fortunate, observing around him how easy it was for the people who did not know, did not wonder, were not convinced, and did not question—prayed to the good God that those foreigners from Buenos Aires would not disturb the peace of the angels and would permit the honoring of those slain by hammer and sickle. In his long moments of solitude, during his walks or in his hotel room, he had sketched and then designed in full engineering detail eight versions of the same monument. He saw it erected by the mass grave, facing east, and portraying not the ordeal but the light that had followed it, not the tears of the living but their gratitude.

The Argentinean anthropologists suffered from a chronic national illness, "los desaparecidos," whose acute, febrile phase had long since burnt itself out. Toddlers or primary-school children when Juan Domingo Perón returned as president after a two-decade exile, when he suddenly died and his last wife,

the third, Isabel Martinez (successor to Eva Duarte, semibeati-
fied and still living, under the name Evita) took over as head of
the republic, innocent bystanders during the period of 355 percent inflation, interminable strikes, demonstrations and attacks
committed by various insurgent factions (which in only one
and a half years led to a death toll of 700), they, those infants,
saw how on March 24, 1975, Lieutenant General Jorge Rafael
Videla, commander of the armed forces and of the junta that
had just staged a coup, installed himself in power and decreed
martial law. While turning into high-school students, and assailed by official speeches regarding the reinstatement of order, they childishly neglected to observe certain developments,
above all the fact that it was possible to speak justifiably of a
decline in visible violence. After all, at that time, until 1978 at
least, they were just kids hypnotized by El Mundial as though
by a boa constrictor, ready to scrap with each other and spend
all their pocket money on T-shirts, watches, stickers, and caps
with pictures of Gauchito. They used to cut out pictures of
their favorite players from the newspapers and magazines.
They gulped down the words of César Luis Menotti. They believed in his gifts as a strategist, in the strong cut of his jaw,
and in his eyes that sparkled like the eternal snows of the Acon-
cagua. And in the summer of '78, when the day circled so long
ago in the calendar finally coincided with the day that had just
begun, and when, toward evening, the referee's first whistle
was heard in Rosario, at that lusterless GFR–Poland no-score
draw, they well and truly lost their heads. Amid the clouds of
confetti that covered not only the stadium stands at each battle
of the national team but also the country itself, beneath those
frenetic and staccato chants (phonetically inimitable, some-

thing like "Ar-hen-tina!!! Ar-hen-tina!!!"), they trembled before the idols who were carving their way toward the supreme trophy. They suffered cruelly at the group defeat to Italy all the more so since one in ten of their compatriots were of Italian origin. They rejoiced with tears as big as lemon seeds at the crushing 6–0 score against Peru (although somewhere, in that anatomically unidentifiable place named the inner forum, or conscience, they felt teardrops of shame at least as big as coffee beans). They shouted until they lost touch with their vocal cords when Mario Kempes, with his flowing locks and puma-like movements, scored the first goal in the final. They cheered the magic passes of Ardiles, the thrusts of Luque, and the slides of Passarella, movements as indescribable as the tango. They gnawed their fingernails to the root when Nanninga equalized for Holland. They exhaled deeply, as though saved from drowning, when Rensenbrink hit the goalpost in the ninetieth minute. They advanced to extra time as though to maturity and entered a state of trance, alongside an entire nation, when the god Kempes (El Goleador) and Bertoni brought the scoreboard to 3–1 and confiscated the Jules Rimet Cup, catapulting Argentineans from the middle of a military regime into the status of world champions. After that unrepeatable moment, in which it would have been impossible to take the pulse because of the speed at which it was racing, in which trainer Menotti was thrown up in the air by his trusty soldiers from the pitch, and a kid (somewhat older than the future anthropologists) sobbed on the turf in the position of reserve player, heeded by none, although he was later to be rechristened El Pibe d'Oro (the Golden Child) in place of his real name, Diego Maradona, and was to enter the gallery of great artists (in alphabetical order, between Mann and Marcello), finally, exactly at that moment, the intoxication of football came to an end. Silence settled after uproar and hubbub. Eyes reaccustomed themselves to surrounding faces, objects, and reality. They blinked in amazement, then consternation and fear, later, terror. Against the backdrop of a decline in visible violence, invisible violence had burgeoned. People were arrested on buses, on busy pavements, in parks, at work, at the tables of bars, in markets, or in the cinema; some were even enjoying a few breaths of familial air in their own homes, especially at night, when they were pulled from between the sheets, forcibly thrust out the door, and thrown into the backs of those vans that enjoyed the reputation of hearses. They never came back. Not the next day, not on Sunday, not the following week, month, or year. And the five high-school students, without knowing each other at the time, without any of them knowing the fate of the others and knowing even less about their own fate, were struck down in that period by the germs of "los desaparecidos," an incurable disease when it involves the disappearance of a father, a beloved teacher, a grandparent, the vendor from the gelateria on the corner, or a neighbor in the habit of giving out sweets to the kids, flying a kite with the boys, and kicking a ball with those whose mustaches were just beginning to sprout. The disease was slow and hidden in its action, like many vicious ailments. It did not attack any of the classic organs, but precisely that anatomically unidentifiable spot named the conscience after the all too sewn-up victory in the match with Peru. Otherwise, for those five (who were still at the stage of being separate fingers and never suspected that they would one day form a hand), that match was turning with every passing day from a piece of idiocy, from a poorly staged farce, into a symbol of superior officers' and Jorge Rafael Videla's mode of being. A visible symbol. But how would an invisible symbol have looked? The answer to that question, the children who now were no longer children but adolescents told themselves, could be provided only by the disappeared, "los desaparecidos," provided they were still alive. However, in March 1981 the waters of the military junta once more grew agitated, ashen, roaring as though on the threshold of a storm. And Videla was dispossessed of the instruments of power by Field Marshal Roberto Viola. Shortly after, while students at lay or Catholic colleges, the five no longer found the field marshal as head of state, because his place had been taken by Lieutenant General Leopoldo Galtieri by means of a conjuring trick. While the national economy resembled a marshy wasteland full of cow pats (and in which bullfights had just taken place under torrential rain), as the disappearance of one, two, fifty, or one hundred Argentineans had been transformed into the disappearance of 30,000, as the 30,000 had at least 300,000 relatives and friends, without taking into account acquaintances, the clergy, merciful souls, defenders of just causes, and the rabble with a taste for noisy demonstrations, as the Republic of Argentina did not number more than thirty-seven million souls, and the rumors, the mourning weeds of the mothers, and the semibeatitude of Eva Perón were more alive than ever, on April 2, 1982, Leopoldo Galtieri wagered on a second great conjuring trick. And the procedure, an extremely complicated one in the contemporary system of international conjuring, worked for him up to a point, because he was relying on the patriotic feeling of his audience—an ardent and edifying feeling, one that was vigorous, without nuance, and unhesitating, one that had been kept in mothballs since the curtain fell on El Mundial. What did 30,000 disappeared matter (maybe they had run off with their mistresses, maybe they had been embezzlers and decided to vanish, maybe they had emigrated, maybe they had just staged their arrests, maybe, maybe, maybe, who can know?), what did they signify compared to the honor and bravado of wresting from the hands of those albino English Las Islas Malvinas, that paradisiacal realm (otherwise quite barren and windswept), whose very name those uppity English had desecrated, changing it to the Falkland Islands? Against such a backdrop, it even became secondary that Osvaldo Ardiles, the midfielder who (uniquely) wore No. 1 on his shirt and in the hearts of all, was giving his best for a London club, Tottenham Hotspur, from whom he now also received his pay-packet. Galtieri was on his high horse, and the sinking of the HMS *Sheffield*, that ultramodern destroyer with Royal Navy insignia, elevated him for a week or two onto a fiery winged stallion, in whose saddle only the legendary Manuel Belgrano, one of the fathers of the nation, had ridden in September 1812 in the battles against the Spanish at Tucumán and Salta. The British generally have a good sense of humor, but not on the battlefield, and in this case (the first war broadcast live on television) they proved downright sullen. Not only did the conjuring trick not amuse them, but they disrupted the lieutenant general's performance to such an extent that he fell off the back of that fiery stallion and into disgrace with his own audience. So it was that on June 14, shortly before the opening of another El Mundial, España '82 (which the titleholders were to exit prematurely, with their tails between their legs), Major General Reynaldo Bignone gravely and dutifully assumed the supreme position of state. However, what no one noticed during the course of Señor Galtieri's second conjuring number, under the fascination of the foaming waves and shrapnel that lapped Las Malvinas, was the pulling off of a third, smaller, less spectacular trick, eclipsed by the grandeur of the one in full view. It had been the destruction, in barracks and on other army premises, under the cover of the war, of the overwhelming majority of the documents relating to the disappeared. It was then that they calmly burned—and the thin plumes of smoke couldn't rival the sulfur and haze of the explosions—tons and tons of papers bearing the stamp TOP SECRET, arrest warrants and execution orders, lists upon lists with the names of those yanked up from among their fellows like weeds or rotten teeth, express recommendations for the personnel in the torture chambers, interrogators' notes and findings, strategies and regulations to erase all trace of the dead, of their biographies, of their identities. Also transformed to ash were the papers that contained the locations of detention centers. Soot was all that remained of the lists of personnel and payrolls, the minutes of junta council and general staff meetings (although the two forums were one), magnetic tapes, photographs, and film reels, even the personal diaries of the officers who had made that terrifying machinery function, a machinery that did not rattle, did not break down, and produced immense quantities of grief. Then the wind blew and the ashes were scattered. Deprived as they were of key information regarding its origin and evolution, in effect left with no clinical records (such as, in the case of other diseases, the results of blood, sputum and urine tests, X-rays, blood pressure readings, etc., etc.), this might be one explanation, one among many, as to why the strange "los desaparecidos" malady took such deep root in the five college students (and in another few million Argentineans) and became incurable. As for Major General Reynaldo Bignone, still preparing the step back from military regime to democracy, cautiously and unhurriedly, leaving enough time to arrange many things and for elections not to be held too hastily, he ascertained one wet October morning, as people were crossing the thresholds of the polling stations, that he had held onto power for sixteen months, that inflation had risen to 900 percent, and that the country's foreign debt (which he personally did not have to pay back) had reached unprecedented levels. He smiled and withdrew into the wings. Entering the scene on that same October day in 1983, but not until toward midnight, after the announcement of the preliminary results of the presidential election, Raúl Alfonsin, leader of the Radical Civic Union, also smiled. Excited by victory, exhausted by electoral campaigning, confident in his abilities and in predestination. The title of doctor lent him something of the optimism of physicians fresh from university benches, who do not doubt that they can cure even hopeless cases. After only two months, CONADEP (La Comisión Nacional para los Desaparecidos) came into being, with ten members appointed by President Alfonsin and another three designated by members of parliament. On December 29, on one of those days when sloth is in full flow, Ernesto Sábato (the writer himself) was unanimously elected leader of that commission, which had no judicial powers, but only the role and the duty of collecting information, examining facts, drawing up periodic reports, and transferring files relating to murders to the courts. And then a less-than-usual phenomenon occurred: although at first it wasted a good few weeks on establishing its own internal departments (Testimonies, Documentation and Data Processing, Procedures, Legal, and, finally, Administrative, a department without which nothing can function), CONADEP did not conform to the customary ways of all commissions that investigate something. More precisely, it did not get lost in thickets of details, it was not transformed into a fencing court (intended for political duels and individual pride), nor did it sweep the gathered dirt under the carpet. Nevertheless, something was still rotten in the state of Argentina. The president of the senate, for instance, unlike his counterpart in the chamber of deputies, disregarded the decree to which the commission owed its existence and refused to be numbered among the midwives and wet nurses of that independent forum, depriving it of the names and expertise of a further three members. What predictably followed was the thrusting of spokes in wheels, spokes of insidious and occult character, ready at any time to impede the cart from advancing and to overturn it. However, it seems that the wheels were strong, in any case much stronger than the spokes, which they broke to pieces, because the first report of CONADEP was printed in 1984, rocking the printing press and the printers, the five students at lay or Catholic colleges (now in their final or penultimate year), and all Spanish-speaking readers. Moreover, that compendium of atrocities was not limited to its native linguistic region, and soon demonstrated to English-speakers, via New York publisher Farrar, Straus, and Giroux and under the title *Never Again* (*Nunca Mas*), that the adjective *terrifying* has limitless content. That text was based on 50,000 pages of testimonies and investigations, which it had compressed into countless individual cases and into a general statement. In the 340 camps destined for opponents of the junta, nameless, isolated, and scattered over a national surface area of 1,727,000 square miles, the chief rules had been inexhaustible brutality and absolute caprice. All those cast into those miniature hells had lived out their days (in fact, their remaining days) bound head and foot, blind because of the hoods that covered their eyes, starved, left to lie in their own excrement or submerged in the soldiers' latrines. It was impossible for the prisoners to communicate with one another, and the maltreatment to which they were subjected betrayed the sexual repression of soldiers deployed to such barren places, it encompassed old methods of the Inquisition, refinements of Asiatic sadism, and new techniques inspired by electric current. One of the ultimate tortures, often employed in the years in which three generals and a field marshal succeeded each other as head of state, had been burial of the exhausted bodies up to the neck, leaving the inert heads in the sun to bake and burst like melons. From the testimonies of the few survivors it emerged that the interrogations were not even aimed at any information in particular, but were merely occasions for gratuitous torture, treated initially as a duty of employment, latterly as a means of driving away boredom and a sport in itself, arousing the imagination, abilities, and passion of the players. At a given moment, however, a serious tactical problem arose: the corpses. For minds which, in the shelter of helmets, had set under way and then perfected that vast penitentiary system (floating unknown above the official courts and prisons), the matter was intended to be solved, and even had been solved for a while, by well-hidden and camouflaged mass graves. But the large, too large, numbers of the dead, surprisingly large even for the strategists of the entire operation, no longer allowed the application of the initial plan. And then, as the report drawn up by CONADEP specified, army aircraft had been taken from their hangars and loaded with fuel, they had been guided to landing strips and filled with a less-than-usual cargo—human bodies in frightful condition: shrunken, wasted, swollen, withered, mangled, tumefied. The airplanes took off (as the pilots declared, recalling that all young boys dream sooner or later of becoming pilots), flew over dry land and a part of the ocean, opened the hatches designed for parachute jumps, and released those bodies from a high altitude, so that they would be swallowed by the waters of the Atlantic. As chance would have it (hence the misgivings of the pilots and their thoughts about the wishes of young boys) some of the dead were not even dead, and their groans and death rattles could be heard clearly in the cockpit before the final drop. And there was something else: the homes of the disappeared had been looted, and their properties sold and resold, which meant that the "los desaparecidos" disease allowed some (not the pilots) to fill their purses and serenely look forward to civilian life after their life in uniform. By the winter of 1984 one after another, the commission managed to make the invisible visible. There was a minute (or perhaps there were many) when the hair stood up on the back of the nation's neck and nostrils forgot to breathe. It was also then that the wails of the mothers were transformed into deafening screams, the faces of the mothers turned as white as mother's milk, and the eyes of the mothers bulged so hard that they seemed to leap from their sockets, shatter in fragments on the cobbles, and burn, like sulfuric acid, whatever they touched. After that minute (or however many there may have been), the politicians prepared pious speeches, dressed in black, cleared their throats in reverse (so that their voices would sound cracked and distraught, rather than ringing and vehement), and showed themselves to the people to demonstrate their state of shock and indignation. The minister of justice gave up his brightly colored ties early on and promised all kinds of things, while the justice system itself, as an apparatus, as a mechanism in permanent function, servile but not insensitive to the name and remarks of a passing minister, made a brief minute's pause (evaluating the situation, seemingly ruminating on the promises), after which it resumed its tireless chasing of its own tail. To the ears of the five college graduates, having now passed the strenuous ordeal of the baccalaureate, there came notions such as the principle of individual (rather than collective) responsibility, the absence of any evidence incriminating certain persons (usually those with many stars on their epaulettes or a stripe on their trousers), the civil courts' lack of competency in cases regarding the military (and what can a raven do to another raven?), the presumption of innocence (when there were so many guilty!), insult to authority (with the consequent trials for calumny), the guarantee of property (even when it had been acquired by dubious means), and so on and so forth, et cetera, and so on, et cetera. Carriers of the "los desaparecidos" virus, the five were more affected by the image of the mothers drained of tears than by the impotence of democracy to break with the past. And they ended up studying at North American universities, alongside hundreds of compatriots suffering from the same malady, all of them specializing in forensic anthropology, whereby they hoped to help in the discovery of the dead in the earth, if not those in the ocean, in identifying them, one by one, so that the sons might at last return home, even if in sealed coffins, and rest in the tombs of their own families, not in the wilderness. Under the cult of the Super Bowl, NBA, and NHL, their jubilation was more restrained when El Pibo d'Oro, now mature and flighty in the summer of 1986, committed a handball (the hand of God, he later said) during a "soccer" match with those uppity English and took his team to the 114,500-spectator final of the Mexican El Mundial in the Aztec Stadium, where through wizardry, with the support of his adjutants Valdano and Burruchaga (both with the forename Jorge), and through uninterrupted communication with Santa Maria Madre de Dios, he subjugated the Germans and hurled the Argentineans once more, this time not from a military regime, but from economic chaos, into the condition of world champions. After that, inflation galloped to 1,200 percent, the rate of unemployment reached boiling point, the initial optimism of President Alfonsin was transformed to rictus, soured, and anguished gestures, and the former United States scholarship students scattered into the interior of that gigantic triangle, whose base is along the Tropic of Capricorn and whose tip is Tierra del Fuego, with its western side along the crests of the Andes and its eastern side along 2,200 nautical miles of the Atlantic coast. They were not to be glimpsed in the large cities or near highways or railroads, for the simple reason that the military junta had sited the mass graves in the most deserted spots. To attempt to meet them was equivalent to looking for a needle in a haystack, because they had lost themselves, along with their incurable disease and their freshly acquired profession, in the limitless pampas, especially in their western, arid part, in the boundless forests of araucaria and austral beech, on the windswept plateaus of Patagonia, on the rain-lashed plain of Gran Chaco, on the slopes of mountains, among the lakes and snows before the eternal glaciers of the south, in the northern areas where the roar of the Iguazu Falls was audible, around concentric, imaginary circles with the Mar Chiquita lagoon at their center. With a certain amount of striving, those investigators who ever groped for bodily remains and caused the disappeared to reappear along with their names and coffins, could be found in village and small-town taverns of an evening, drinking and listening to rock, chatting, wishing to sleep easily and soundly. After years and years of rummaging around a triangle that measured 1,727,000 square miles and which had been christened the Land of Silver, long after Carlos Menem (as a pureblood Peronist president) had tamed inflation, the budget deficit, the balance of payments, and other suchlike abstractions, afterward higgledy-piggledy bringing them back, shortly after Menem had ceded power to Fernando de la Rua and after the consummation of three footballing banquets (Coppa del Mondo, the World Cup, and La Coupe du Monde), one of the teams of anthropologists, a five-fingered hand, arrived one morning at Buenos Aires airport to board a plane to a small European country, controlled by the Soviets for a few decades, to give their diagnosis on another mass grave. They had been invited there by a government with plenty of flies in its ointment (a whole swarm could be glimpsed between the lines of the diplomatic letters, it was almost as though you could hear the buzzing), but also by the former political prisoners, who trusted in their neutrality and discernment. The two women in the group went to the toilet before takeoff and relieved themselves. The men did not bother, because the plane had a cubi-

cle. On the other hand, they left behind on a seat in the airport
a number of newspapers and an open parenthesis: up to that
profligate night between millennia, named for a time December 31, 1999, and, after the chimes of cathedral clocks and mad
salvoes of fireworks, January 1, 2000, when twenty-four years
had elapsed since the coup by Lieutenant General Jorge Rafael
Videla and seventeen years since the smile of Major General
Reynaldo Bignone, no one, absolutely no one had been in-
dicted or convicted for the conscious spreading of the "los desaparecidos" virus, for the grief of the mothers or for the infection of so many consciences.

→>◂←

I hung up my yellow anorak in the window, the signal for Jojo,
and she appeared at around nine. She was amazed, she had seen
us getting out of the taxi, but not into the ambulance, because
we had agreed that she should not visit me after Paulina returned, that we should meet for a time in town at the archaeologists' house and in our places in the woods, until I convinced
Auntie to take in a new lodger, a lady lodger, who would also
live in my room, where a nuptial photograph with the crest
"I. F. Kissling, Ploesci, Photo-Globe" hung upon the wall and
where there was but one bed. I told Jojo what had happened,
how the voyage only seemed to have come to an end, how it
might have become an eternal voyage, with a certificate from
the coroner, rather than a passport. Her lips parted slightly; her
upper lip became thinner and her lower lip quivered. Jojo shook
her head and spoke sweetly. We had to help Auntie to get better and to laugh, to fulfill as many of her wishes as we could; in
the end she was the mistress of the house and our friend, and

she deserved to get well. The luggage from Greece we left untouched in the vestibule, and the table laid as though for a festive occasion ("the meezonplass, dear," as Auntie Paulina would have said) remained intact, except for the joint of veal, cooked for a lunch or dinner with her, which ended up as our breakfast. We sat cross-legged on the carpet, eating slices of meat, toasted bread, and yogurt directly from the tray. Then I stretched out, looking at the ceiling, ashamed that I had not been waiting for Auntie with an umbrella, that I had not hired a taxi for the whole day, that I had not called for an ambulance sooner, that she, who had asked me to be patient for the presents, who wanted to tell me about everything under the moon and stars, had lost the tan from her cheeks. I was talking my head off, I described the ambitions of the stretcher-bearer, the doctor's agitation, the neon light, and the notices, I allowed the film sequence I had imagined in front of the closed door of the emergency room to unreel once again, I even remembered the number of chairs I had lined up in military fashion using the toe of my shoe. Jojo claims that all of a sudden I fell silent, without finishing my thought about the crooked heart and the peevish dog, that I twisted round onto my stomach and fell asleep like a log.

And my sleep came to an end like this: her left palm climbed and descended under my T-shirt, up and down my back, the fingers of her right hand pitter-pattered over my crown and down my nape. In three quarters of an hour, Jojo had collected and packed a whole lot of things—two nightshirts, a dressing gown, a wool sweater, a prayer book, underwear, slippers, soap, towels, a comb, a mirror, a knitted cap, a mug and a plate, cutlery, handkerchiefs, a pen and a writing pad. On top she placed a deck of cards. She showed me it with a smile, saying

that whenever her grandmother was in the hospital the cards
had proved to be the most important item of all. When we left
I also removed the roses from the water. Given how the sun
was blazing and the clouds were gathering, another torrential
lunchtime downpour was on the way. Paulina was still sleeping. It was incredible just how much she had slept. In the vein
in the crook of her arm a needle was embedded, to the needle
was connected a thin tube, the other end of the tube was connected to a transparent bag, the bag was hanging from a metal
stand, and the only thing moving was the liquid in the bag,
which slowly slid through the tube into the vein. We sat on the
edge of the bed. Jojo in particular hastened to sit down. Later,
she found a jar on a shelf. She rinsed it and put the roses in it.
She arranged Paulina's things in the drawer of the nightstand
in silence, then mixed some warm water with a drop of vinegar and wiped Auntie's cheeks, chin, and temples. A nurse, not
the same one as on the nightshift, entered at one point with a
thermometer and, as she also was not adverse to a small bribe,
she provided us with a list of light and nourishing foodstuffs,
a kind of diet for pneumonia. Jojo remained in the room, and
I went to a restaurant to fetch some chicken soup, in which I
would have liked, and would have paid for, copious chunks
of meat to float. Outside, the sun was no longer torrid. It had
been swallowed by the clouds, black heavy clouds, which were
drooping, merging, and giving birth to other clouds, also black
and heavy. I did not see the first streak of lightning, but the
thunderclap caught up with me on the steps of a bistro that had
good food. The kitchen made me what I asked, and poured the
soup into a light jug, with a lid, which I promised to return that
evening. My umbrella shielded me from a cold shower but did

not protect my trousers and shoes, which got drenched. In the meantime, Paulina had woken up. She was chattering hoarsely, dressed in one of the nightshirts we had brought, with the knitted cap on her head. She was complaining that, with such a diagnosis, hydrazine would not be lacking and she would put on a fair bit of weight (twenty pounds, to be precise, by her calculations). She took her hand from between Jojo's and called me over to the bed. She was as white as the sheet and sweating. Auntie had not changed. It was as if pneumonia had been part of the schedule of her trip to Greece after all and now its turn had come. She explained to us which bag contained the presents, and how and to whom we should give them out. She wanted to telephone her sister Lucica, who might be upset at her not asking for help and imagine who knows what, and then turn up furious at the hospital. Auntie swallowed a few spoonfuls of soup, coughed, and decided that some acacia honey would do her good. Then she asked us, with her mouth full, whether we would not be too cramped in the bed in my room.

⊰⊱

One of the symptoms of the "los desaparecidos" disease, observed by many who did not realize that it was the sign of a malady, was that the Argentinean anthropologists used to spend their evenings in beer gardens, bars, or pubs, from which they would emerge late at night. They preferred the beer gardens, although in that mountain town, after dusk, one needed long trousers and sweaters. They retreated to closed spaces with low ceilings and thick cigarette smoke only when thrust there by the rain, a biting wind, a chill that mistook the middle of summer for winter, or when one of those whom they had befriended and with whom they had so much to discuss insisted. They drank only spirits. One of the women sometimes drank beer, the one with chestnut hair and many bronze bracelets, but she used to mix it with rum. Everywhere, they were happy with the music, whatever flowed from the speakers. On a few occasions it nonetheless happened that the tall one with the cross would get up from the table, whisper to the barman and, who knows how or by means of the words of which language, he would get him to play "Black Magic Woman" by Santana. They tried to find out a multitude of things about this different kind of junta, one that had kept its military insignia hidden beneath flat caps and proletarian garb, that had not used small, camouflaged detention centers, but huge prisons and labor camps, that had lost count of the dead, although the dead often bore illustrious names, that had been capable of sending a football team to a World Cup only once, in '70, when the adventure had come to an end after the group matches and its star, Gîscanu (El Ganso — The Goose), had not played at all. A junta that demolished churches, that had confiscated even the bakeries and the air people breathed, that in its own way had done something similar to what Castro had done, but more harshly, for a longer time, and with Moscow much closer. The bones left behind by the two juntas were much alike — there were no guilty in either case, as if they had dissolved into thin air. The new politicians resembled hyenas and foxes. In both hemispheres, the people quickly forgot. Compassion and rage shared the fate of autumn flowers, upon which settles hoarfrost: they had faded, withered, then died under the weight of rent, prices, inflation, soap operas and talk shows, family life, victories and defeats in the stadiums. Today and tomorrow counted more than yesterday and the day before, and the politicians referred above all to the day after tomorrow. Just as every individual has his peculiarities, so too had each junta: one had invented "reeducation," setting one pack of rabid prisoners on the other, encouraging sadism as though it were patronizing the arts (for instance, in the penitentiary of a town on the plain, later known for the dribbling skills of the Goose and for the splendor of its tulips); the other had discovered a funereal conjuring trick, making corpses disappear shortly after the fluttering of flags on the army's runways, when the airplanes reached the open ocean and opened their parachute hatches. A wealth of details, nuances, chronologies, and biographical passages were contained in those discussions, in which two worlds met, many glasses were drained, and a number of ashtrays overflowed. As ever, words spoken by day did not have the incandescence of nocturnal sentences. Deeds done by the light of day seemed puny next to the ideas that came after the onset of darkness. One morning, an Argentinean, the one who had appeared at the Roman fort wearing a fringed T-shirt, had the impression that there was something not quite right with the bones of the hands. He examined the hundreds of bags in which the prosecutors had sealed the evidence, he turned them on every side, and lined them up in trays. His professional meticulousness and visual experience all at once touched like two electric wires, the contact produced sparks, and the sparks caused him to start all over again, for the eighth time that week, but this time with a precise aim. And, gradually, the feeling that something was not as it should be became a certainty. From among the bones and fragments of bone inventoried by the military magistrates, the bones of the little fingers were missing. He gave a short whistle, in a manner hard to imitate, and the former gymnasium school pupils of the summer in which Mario Kempes had pierced through clouds of confetti to reach the sky where there reigned a golden statue, the Jules Rimet Cup, now clenched together like the fingers of a hand, in this other summer. The five had acquired the reflex of forming a hand or a fist a long time ago, and it was triggered by the presence of as yet unidentified bodily remains. So a whistle from one of them, used in difficult situations, the same whistle for all, immediately brought them together in the minuscule, rectangular space that had once represented a Roman garrison in an unsafe region. They convinced themselves that this fluke was indeed a fact. They consulted among themselves, and decided not to divulge to anyone else what to them was as clear as day. Then, after darkness fell, at the table of a beer garden with white lanterns, elbow to elbow with three archaeologists and the girlfriend of the one in the checked shirt, they reeled off countless theories, they imagined scenarios, they drank vodka and tequila, they discussed the matter in every shape and form. The whistle and their haste to assemble had, however, caused an agitation before lunch. The coroner, the prosecutors, the lieutenant of the gendarmes, the policeman, the reporters, and a few soldiers had interrupted their business (leafing through the newspapers, as the lieutenant was doing, being not so much a business as an occupation). They had gazed at the Argentineans carefully. Some of them had approached and asked questions. They were, of course, interested in whether the investigators had found something new in the sealed bags. A prosecutor, the captain, insistently offered his services, not suspecting that they had dealt with dozens of lizards like him before, always in uniform, always amiable and cunning, and striving to get under their skin. The Argentineans had quenched general curiosity by saying that it was nothing important, merely an anatomical anomaly. The woman with the chestnut hair and bronze bracelets had whispered to the captain, as if slightly embarrassed at the revelation, that she had seen a pubic bone much larger than any that had so far been inventoried. Then the prosecutors had gone off to eat at Chez Matilda, the Argentineans to the archaeologists' house, where the doctor had cooked zucchini soup and a stew on the gas-canister stove. The chief of police had gone home, and the gendarmes had stretched out on the grass and opened some cans. In the afternoon, each of the five foreigners had seemed preoccupied with something else. One had redone his measurements, jotting down the dimensions of the mass grave in a notebook. Another had taken soil samples and studied them under a microscope. One of the women had employed the tools and substances of a field chemistry laboratory, dripping acids and bases onto splinters of bone, immersing entire bones in reactive solutions. The other had dedicated herself to the written records, summarizing their notes up to that point. The fifth had strolled among the soldiers, watching how they detached the bones of those nameless and ageless dead from the earth and compacted strata. All five, in spite of appearances, had, however, been concentrating on one thing only: finding out whether, in the virgin area of the mass grave, so far untouched by the trowels of the gendarmes, there were bones of little fingers. And there were. Neither more nor less than the bones of other fingers. Consequently it was clear (as they later concluded, by the light of the white lanterns in the beer garden) that the hands had not been mutilated before burial. The fingers were vanishing now, in the present, and the detective story with which they were faced was one without alibis and false trails. The first to touch the bones were the soldiers, but they were eliminated from the discussion because they could never have distinguished the bones of the little finger from those of the ring finger or forefinger, because they were too many, an entire platoon, and they could not have managed to be so united, capable of not uttering a single word, of not being detected. The bones then reached the tables of the young prosecutors, in full sunlight, where they were studied under a magnifying glass, separated, and placed in transparent bags. But they were not the perpetrators either. At another table, at night, a table surrounded by people used to rummaging in the earth (anthropologists, archaeologists, and a girl who helped her grandmother with the gardening), the following arguments had been advanced: the prosecutors lacked a motive to steal the little fingers; if they, nonetheless, had a motive, it would have been impossible for them to identify, separate, and appropriate so many bones, since they were almost constantly supervised by the coroner and the chief of police; supposing that the coroner and the chief of police were also involved, then their acting talents deserved high praise, so well did they simulate poor relations with their accomplices and hatred toward each other; allowing for the possibility of theater, one nonetheless came up against the prejudices of the journalists and their care not to let the young prosecutors out of their sight; moreover, the case plunged into the absurd, for it was a question of finger bones, not diamonds. As for the magistrate colonel, he coordinated and checked everything. It was upon his table that sooner or later everything that emerged from the mass grave arrived. He classified the bones. He sealed the transparent bags. Alone. He did not accept any assistance or company. He was old and had seen much. No one checked up on him. There were plenty of men higher up on the ladder of military justice who had authorized him to conduct the investigations and who could have called him to account, but they had not set foot at the site. And besides sharp cheekbones, the colonel had another peculiarity: a missing finger, the little finger of his left hand. One day, when the temperature hit thirty-four degrees, and the colonel, drenched in sweat, had undone the knot of his necktie and opened the first three buttons of his shirt, they had noticed how much he treasured his lost finger—he wore it around his neck, attached to a silver chain, like an amulet.

So who could the culprit be?

The question was never heard at their table—not because of the volume of the music, a bland FM—but because they all knew the answer. When the radio station clock chimed twelve times, the magistrate colonel turned into a mouse, a sullied hamster, with whom they could play at will. With a twig, they thrust him before a plenary court, but he was shaking like a reed; out of pity, they took him from the dock of the accused and walked him through a number of editorial offices to be photographed and filmed, but he wet himself when the flash bulbs went off and the studio lights came on; they spared him the trauma of media exposure, especially since he was staining the carpets of major press offices, and they took him instead to a pet shop for small animals, so he could see what life was like in a cage, could look other mice in the eye and squeak something, but he gazed at the floor and did not say a word, he had become completely limp; they tethered him with a little collar, a hamster leash, and they dragged him outside, because he no longer reacted to the light flicks of the twig. Frightened, he sniffed the pavement, the gutter. He bumped into an apple core and continued on his way; probably in a different situation he would have nibbled it stalk and all. Then he tried to flee, to find a hiding place. The leash stretched like a piece of elastic, he was stalking something in the drains, in the trash cans, in the holes in the asphalt, in backyards, under a parked car, and it was definitely not a cat. Just as they had removed him from the dock of the accused, now they stuffed him into a bag and later, when they remembered about him, they let him loose among the glasses of vodka and tequila, tethering him to a bottle of mineral water. He ran in circles around the table, mad with hunger. They took a paper napkin, they wrote on it that he must return the little fingers, and gave it to him to gnaw on. Then, as it was nearing one o'clock, they got up to leave, and the mouse disappeared, becoming a sleeping man of law, in room 211 of the hotel.

But the real problem remained. The Argentineans had crossed the ocean and the equator as arbiters of a controversial exhumation in a small country, which on the map looked like a flatfish, with its mouth toward the center of the continent and its tail pressed to a sea, a country which, after the twilight of their junta, had sent three football teams to the World Cup, once allowing them, by collective hypnosis, to tame Gabriel Omar Batistuta and defeat the white-and-blue shirts. They had hoped, even from the right bank of the Rio de la Plata estuary, from the airport, and for the length of the flight that the bodily remains, by their age and provenance, would not disappoint the people who did not deserve to be deceived. And things had turned out exactly the opposite. From the very first day, they had been convinced that the bones had reached or were about to reach the age of two centuries. They did not say so straightaway. A torrential downpour was necessary to make them huddle into a basement bar with the archaeologists who had long since descended to that cellar and were depleting its reserves of wine. One of the Argentineans, the owner of the vest with the face of the Pope, had a passion for chiromancy and he had studied their palms for a time. From what he observed, the seekers of Roman relics were at an impasse. He understood from the archaeologists' accounts that they had located the fort's armory with difficulty, they had been just a step away from discovering its interior and inventory, they were about to see and touch swords, armor, spears, and daggers from the age of the Antonines, when they had been thwarted by a policeman who seemed to have the brain of a guinea fowl, but in fact had the cunning of a wolf. Major Maxim had sniffed the mass grave for a short while, he had seen the bones in it as a huge bone to be gnawed, he had pricked up his ears, not to what the historians had to say, but to what might possibly be said about him. He had then clamped his jaws around that bone and allowed himself to be conquered by his auditory imagination, unleashing the madness of those bones, the disputes, the suspicions, and the passions. What was worse, he had also stirred up expectations in a country twenty-one and a half times smaller than the Republic of Argentina, a country that not long ago had known prisons, but had lost count of the dead, where memory had briefly been awakened from slumber, and where the flies in the ointment of the government stubbornly refused to fly away. And now they, even they, the five seekers of vanished bodies, would have to tell that nice old man who sometimes accompanied them to the beer garden, but who went to bed early, who had spoken French even behind bars, that no monument could be erected next to the mass grave. The victims of the junta could not be honored at the last resting place of the plague dead.

CHAPTER NINE

✦

THE ARTICLE THAT DESCRIBED Onufrie conducting a service at the edge of the mass grave had amounted to fourteen lines and had been squeezed in among sundry summer news items on a page overrun with advertisements. It is likely that his connection with the newspapers would have begun and ended there, had the article not closed with a quotation, a phrase he uttered countless times a day, reproduced without abridgement or addition. Thanks to that unusual pronouncement, other articles had also been printed, about the monastery he was building at Red Rock, about the chapel next to the pine tree with nine crowns, about the scars accumulated on his forefinger, about his straw hat, about his obedient disciples, about his habit of reading on a sunny slope in the afternoons, about his drawling manner of talking, about how he mixed the paints and cleaned the brushes, about his hut, and about a multitude of things that each added one more brushstroke to his portrait. Onufrie had kept silent about many past events: the years of his childhood, the scissors-prick to the left thigh of the Holy Infant, the escape from the mine, the writing of a Gospel on spruce bark, his friendship in the mountains with the man who hid his face yet bore himself like Saint George, the burial of a bear in a park in the largest city, his discussions with the girl in the cart, Sandica, and his nocturnal terrors and wanderings, when it seemed to him his days grew grim. In his turn, the carpenter's mate, though assailed by the questions and curiosity of true-believers, had not breathed a word about the bluish-black tuft on the father's crown. Even so, around the monk a legend was woven, which caught him in its strands like a loom. A long article, influenced a great deal by the language and epic constructions of the *Lives of the Saints,* written by a young man who had hidden his real intent, while wielding a shovel at the foundations of the future monks' cells and sleeping together with the disciples, contributed to the dissemination of Onufrie's name and deeds. The weekly in which that piece of reportage came out dealt with natural cures, cosmetic and culinary recipes, formulas for rapid weight loss, hair regeneration, and treatment of acne, it explored subjects such as lack of sexual appetite and failure to achieve orgasm, it recommended books and music, lines of clothing and travel, it offered advice on being a success in society at intimate soirées, and on staying on good terms with your boss, it never avoided astrological predictions and devoted itself in a distinct way to the Orthodox calendar and religious events with an excess of piety and a great eagerness to see celestial signs and miracles wherever its reporters might alight. And so it had been in the case of Onufrie: the photograph that showed the monk with a straw hat shaking his right forefinger, the illustration of the small chapel and the church clad with scaffolding. The moving story of the descents of the Virgin were reinvented, the first being Her decent to the sanatorium, at night, in the middle of a storm, when the Holy Mother had apparently glided down on a streak of lightning, touched the knees of the paralytic, and taught him to walk again, the second happening in the clearing at Red Rock, when

She was supposed to have marked the spot of the future monastery with a thunderbolt from the sun and traced on the ground the outline of the walls, and the third linked with the mass grave, when the Mother of God had whispered to the monk to come down from the mountain and bless the bones spewed up amid the ruins of the fort. This account, stretching over two pages of the magazine, also contained a host of fictive images, such as the flock of doves that often roosted on the roof of the chapel, or the crack in the trunk of the pine tree, which resembled the profile of Mary. Such stories contained in such a publication, especially in summer, when people are on vacation and like to travel, when the days are long and warm, had in many respects changed Onufrie's life. To the clearing came women flushed and perspiring after having made their way through the forest, hoping that the steep ascent would serve as penance and wipe away many sins. Along came men, irritated and skeptical, also exhausted by the steep slope, thirsty and wishing to smoke. Along came children, noisy and boisterous, happy to clamber up the heaps of sand and on the scaffolding, to rip up the flowers at the door to the chapel, to splash in the icy water of the spring, to shout and whistle, to throw stones at the dogs. The women wanted to see with their own eyes what they had read or heard. They scouted around, they whispered, they tried to discover the traces and the lingering presence of miracles. They lit candles, made genuflections, knelt and filled their breasts with the air perfumed by the incense of the Immaculate Virgin's passage and protection. They took away Eucharist bread and holy water, they left lists of names to be remembered in prayers, and they made donations to the building of the holy monastery according to their pocket and their soul, also according to their pride. Some put money in the poor box, others obstinately insisted on being included on the list of founders or on giving the money directly to the father. They all had something to tell him before asking his blessing. They all made plaints, implored him, told him stories, thanked him, asked his advice, scrounged teachings. In their masses, they had driven out the tranquility of the place; they had changed its rhythms, sounds, customs, and décor. The flow of visitors, which had begun to trickle since the very first appearance of the fourteen-line article and swelled as other articles appeared, had not died out like a sudden and passing torrent, but had settled into its own streambed, like a brook that would never run dry no matter what the season. And this stream wearied Onufrie, who could not avoid its path. The monastery was the work of the Mother of the Holy Child, Her will, which he had awaited for almost half a century, patiently, humbly, hopefully, until patience, humility, and hope had moulted and become frail, moving Her only then, because She had different criteria from mortals, a different time, and different units of measure. Had he built the hermitage of his own will, he would have sought another shelter for himself and left it to others to finish, monks eager to bathe in the stream, monks to whom it did not seem that the days were growing grim. But the love of an old man surpasses all other loves. And as a tool in Her fashioning hands, he could not permit himself to leave. He put up with it and got used to it. He was forced to do things he had never foreseen, to station a disciple at the door when he was praying and when he was resting, to bless ten minced loaves and a barrel of water so that there would be enough for all at Eucharist, to place at the entrance of the chapel two huge trays, (the grass was becoming blackened from the candles), to read reams of names for remembrance, and to shrive souls until morning, to keep a dog on a chain, a shaggy white dog, the fiercest, to ask that another deep and capacious latrine be dug, to put a stop to all kinds of aberrations on the part of the believers, because they, even if they had never seen the flock of doves or the profile of Mary, used to toss breadcrumbs onto the roof of the chapel, until wheat began to sprout between the laths, until the eaves became clogged and the ground filled with the droppings of birds. And to the branches of the pine with nine crowns they tied so many icons, wreaths, crosses, photographs of the sick, and letters with prayers that it had turned into a kind of Christmas tree. They filled their pockets with pebbles from the ballast of the foundations, convinced that they guarded against evil, brought good luck, and healed illness. Finally, to straighten what was growing so crookedly, one torrid day Onufrie slammed the door of his cell, raised the forefinger of his right hand, and uttered emphatically, not drawlingly, that *thrice has the Mother of God descended from the heavens to show Her succor and faith to Onufrie.* And silence fell, interrupted only by the shaggy white dog on its chain, when the priest unbound it with his own hand and promised aloud that he would never bind it again. And the dog broke into a run, ran in a circle, bumped the skirts of Onufrie's soutane with its head and tail, whimpered and fawned, ran with its tongue lolling to one side, its ears flapping, jumped up with its forelegs onto his chest, licked his beard, and chewed apart one of his laces. Then the disciples combed the roof, raked and swept around the chapel, climbed a ladder and cleaned the pine tree. They labored until it grew dark, and for a short while, as long as the ashen light lasted, the clearing at

Red Rock looked as it had before that fourteen-line article. For the monk who had survived eighty years and paralysis, the shadows of dusk joined with the things untouched by the flood of people. He prayed in his hut and threatened the north wall with his forefinger. He awoke speaking to the Immaculate Virgin. He awoke once more weeping. He fed the dogs with his own hand. He cropped his bluish-black tuft every four hours and burned the bunches of hair, so that they would not be found and treated as relics. He wrote hymns to the Holy Virgin on dried spruce bark, using a quill and bilberry juice. Sometimes he went outside at night, on tiptoe, to stretch out in the grass and gaze up at the curtain of stars behind which slept the Virgin. Sometimes he went to watch the sunrise. And one morning, when the sun had not yet risen above the wooded peak across the valley, he saw on the pine tree some large caps of trunk rot, fixed neither too high nor too low, so that they could be seen by eyes that understood their meaning.

→>-<←

In the end, the tenses of the verbs settled into a common groove, the persons of the narrators, first and third (the latter with so many variants and identities), became one, and events thronged toward a day that began uncertainly and remained undecided, with a light gray film covering the sky. Auntie Paulina, whose temperature had come under control and into whose treatment hydrazine had been introduced, said that there had not been such an insufferable day for a long time, that it was as though something were weighing her head down on the pillow, that she had a tingling in her arms and legs. She asked her sister Lucica to fan her with a newspaper, and prayed for two or three drops of rain to fall, to get rid of the atmospheric pressure.

However, she jumped up as though scalded when she found out that in her cupboard, among the sweaters, an envelope had appeared, with her lodger's name inscribed on it in large rounded letters, and containing twenty gold coins. "You're a mule, a mule in flesh and blood," she shouted at Petrus at around twelve o'clock, when he arrived alone with a full lunch pail. She sipped the dumpling soup and scolded him for not having accepted the gift. She quickly chewed the pieces of steak and boiled vegetables and could not understand where so much stubbornness came from. She poured her fury out on the archaeological site, and at last, licking her fingers after the apple pie, she said that a wedding gift cannot be refused. And she fell asleep with a cold compress on her brow, and the rosy image of a wedding no one had thought of. Outside it was stifling. The military prosecutors did not sit down for a moment. They closely supervised the soldiers. They asked for trowels and worked elbow to elbow with them. They consulted with each other and made many notes. They could not understand why, on that morning, so many little-finger bones kept appearing. However, they could not report the situation or receive any orders, because their chief was missing. According to the platoon on the third shift, the colonel had received a telephone call that night and left room 211 before daybreak. At the archaeologists' house, on the other hand, they were all sitting down. From the veranda they watched the bustle at the mass grave and drank tea without sugar. They didn't rise from their chairs until lunchtime. They fried some fish and opened a bottle of champagne, to clink glasses with the Argentineans (though they had to be content with cups and mugs) at their last meal there. In the afternoon, at an improvised press conference in a small hall in the hotel, the five had presented their conclusions. As foreign observers called upon to give a verdict on any possible fraud involving the bones, they were of the opinion that the dead who had been tumbled together into that grave had lived long before the proclamation of the people's republic, even long before the first king had come to the throne, during an epoch in which Commander Manuel Belgrano, in another land, had not yet crushed the Spaniards at the battles of Tucamán and Salta and in which plagues, especially the bubonic plague, had ravaged both hemispheres. They added that their opinion was only consultative in nature and that the final verdict was to be given by the official investigators, who had yet to conclude their research. In the room it was stuffy, and that aged gentleman in a linen suit hastened outside, very pale, mopping his brow with a handkerchief and seeking a glass of water. Before that day came to an end, he tore into eight pieces his designs for a monument, tossed the paper into the toilet, and flushed the water twenty-three times. Not on that night, but the next, it drizzled and the wind blew. Among the walls of the fort slipped a figure. Perhaps it was a dog. It moved forward a little, noiselessly, it listened, it stole on, and approached the only sentinel. It must have sensed from the rhythm of his breathing or the position of his body that the soldier was sleeping. Then it went in the opposite direction, still with quick and cautious movements. It stopped at the edge of the mass grave. It was not a dog. It was a man who moved with short swift steps. He emerged from his hiding place, trod carefully over the bones, and scattered over them something from a little sack. It was so dark that the figure not only had no face but also cast no shadow. In the morning, they discovered the first old and rusted bullets, fragments of bone that bore the mark of those bullets, even a skull still containing the bullet that had perforated the forehead and implanted itself in the cranium. Also that morning, Onufrie was to hear the confession of a man he had never seen or heard, but whom he had long ago shriven by letter.